About the author

After the success of her first book *Ellie Hopeson 91* which was published by Pegasus in 2018 when she herself was ninety-one, Muriel Freeborn has embarked on another story.

Not able to garden or go for long walks, she has found writing a great pleasure. Combined with her joy of music making with friends, her days are full of interest in things around her.

She has been widowed for many years and has a son on the verge of retirement.

LIVING IN HARMONY

Muriel Freeborn

LIVING IN HARMONY

Vanguard Press

VANGUARD PAPERBACK

© Copyright 2020
Muriel Freeborn

The right of Muriel Freeborn to be identified as author of
this work has been asserted by her in accordance with the
Copyright, Designs and Patents Act 1988.

All Rights Reserved

No reproduction, copy or transmission of this publication
may be made without written permission.
No paragraph of this publication may be reproduced,
copied or transmitted save with the written permission of the
publisher, or in accordance with the provisions
of the Copyright Act 1956 (as amended).

Any person who commits any unauthorised act in relation to
this publication may be liable to criminal
prosecution and civil claims for damages.

A CIP catalogue record for this title is
available from the British Library.

ISBN 978 1 78465 747 5

*Vanguard Press is an imprint of
Pegasus Elliot MacKenzie Publishers Ltd.*
www.pegasuspublishers.com

First Published in 2020

**Vanguard Press
Sheraton House Castle Park
Cambridge England**

Printed & Bound in Great Britain

Acknowledgement

GO GET ORGANISED, Bath, for typing.

Chapter 1

I have never forgotten Maudie, which is odd, because I cannot recall what she looked like, whether or not she was taller than I was, or plumper, what colour her hair was, whether it was curly or straight, I cannot recall her voice. I just know that when I was five years old, Maudie was my friend.

We both lived in a cul-de-sac of council houses up north. My father was one of three families who owned a car, but Maudie's family was not one of them. Our houses were semi-detached. Mine was on the left of a pair, and Maudie's house was on the right of a pair further down the road. When I visited, I was conscious of every room, the hall and stairway, being the other way around.

I remember her birthday; it was the seventh of August. I was invited to tea once and I can only think that it was to celebrate her birthday. I often wonder, when the day comes around, if she is still alive.

We played together, we probably attended the same school, although I have no memory of that. I have a vivid memory of us both going to play with someone who lived at the end of the cul-de-sac, and we were firmly told to go home as it was dinnertime. I arrived back first, and Maudie ran down the road to her house. A clear memory of such a small incident.

I cannot remember if her home was well furnished, but it was my good fortune to glimpse their front room, where we were never allowed to play, through the half-open door.. To my great delight, I saw that Maudie's mother had a piano.

"We've got one of those," I remember announcing.

"Sissy gives lessons," Maudie's mother replied.

Whether or not Sissy was a member of the family, or whether she hired the front room for her teaching, I do not know. The fact that Maudie lived in a house with a piano was enough for me to think she was special. All my relations had a piano, ours belonged to my grandfather who had died before I was born. My mother played hymns and my father played with her on his violin, which also came from grandfather. When I told my mother that Sissy taught the piano, she did not hesitate to pay for me to have lessons.

Sissy was stern. I remember the many trips I made to Maudie's house on my own with my music case, often in the dark, to knock at the front door and be ushered into that sacred space, to learn my notes, and play the *Stephanie Gavotte*. I didn't see Maudie on those occasions, I don't think she had lessons.

Even so, I was very fond of Maudie, we never fell out, we just played in our own gardens and in the gardens of children I don't remember. The cul-de-sac was always very quiet in the 1930's. The older children played at skipping and top spinning in the road.

It is surprising that I remember her, as when I was six years old, my father, who was a civil servant, was moved miles away to the south coast. I broke the news to Maudie's mother, explaining that I would no longer be able to play with her, as we were moving too far away. I remember feeling very grown up when I told her. It was an important topic of conversation at home. I don't know if Maudie was sad or not.

Throughout our play times together, she made me aware that I could know someone, outside our family, on a personal level. Maudie was mine to talk about and to trust, I felt safe in her company. I am glad that she still lives in my memory.

Chapter 2

It didn't seem at all curious to me that our next home was at the top of a cul-de-sac, another semi-detached house on the left of the pair, painted white with light green woodwork, just right for the seaside. It was definitely smarter than our previous abode and had a garage for the car.

There was a large garden extending from the side of the house, with several fully-grown trees. It was all quite wild and rose steeply to a high fence at the top. There was a small garden at the back of the house overlooking a bungalow.

As I was getting my bearings, exploring the new surroundings soon after our arrival, a young girl looked over the fence and asked me my name. She said her name was Flo.

It took no time at all for her to tell me that her mother worked at the big house hidden away through the trees beyond our garden. She explained that all the houses in our cul-de-sac were built on land belonging to Miss Grantley, and that the said lady owned the bungalow in which she lived with her mother.

I was impressed by the way she spoke, so fluently, and her eagerness to establish a welcoming friendship. She seemed very mature to me. In the course of a rather one-sided conversation, I was informed that I was probably going to the same local school she attended.

I quietly warmed to that information, as I was very apprehensive at starting a new school in the junior department, now that I had just reached the age of seven. The fact that I could say I lived next door to Flo, was a good starting point in conversation, especially as she was one of the older girls. I felt pleased that she had spoken to me at all.

After her introduction, she quickly retreated, through the backdoor, and I turned to look for my mother to tell her Flo lived in the bungalow and went to the same school that I was going to attend. Flo, of course, went in search of her mother to announce the sparse pieces of information that she had been able to glean from me.

The way to my new school was farther than the distance I had to walk up north. It wasn't necessary for me to cross a main road, but I did have to walk along one a fair way, before branching off down another busy road, which I did have to cross. My mother never accompanied me to school, as far as I can remember, even when I was five years old, as it was very close to where we lived, there were always children from our road who walked alone. The information Flo had given her mother prompted the offer of a short cut over the dividing fence through the garden of the bungalow, thus cutting off the need to walk down our cul-de-sac and along the main road. That became the arrangement. Climbing the fence was made easy and Flo would take me to school.

At first she took the part of the elder sister, accompanying me there by nine o'clock, home for lunch and back again for the afternoon lessons. I was grateful for her company and put up with her occasional bossiness. She made the introduction to a new routine, where my northern accent stood out, much easier. My good musical ear soon dampened any broad pronunciation and smoothed my speech to blend in quite quickly with other children.

I don't think I missed Maudie. I soon made friends with girls in my class. We were all exposed to the strict discipline of Miss Beale, and clung to each other when she was displeased with one or other of us, all of us at times. I know I secretly longed to go up to the next class, in the hope that my failings would be dealt with more kindly.

Flo became a firm fixture in my life. I admired her down to earth attitude, her ability to make decisions and to know the answers to any situation that arose, whether or not to join in playground arguments, and whether to avoid certain older children. Flo wasn't afraid of anyone. I watched her from afar at playtimes as she mixed with her peers. I never saw her father, and I didn't ask about him. Her mother was very kindly towards me. I did notice that the bungalow was simply furnished; there were no ornaments or pictures, and sadly, there was no piano.

I remember going to a pantomime with Flo and her mother one Christmas, and coming back to spend the night at the bungalow. Flo came home singing one of the songs we were all encouraged to join in, during the pantomime, but to my horror the song was barely recognisable, as her singing was way off key. I found it unbearable, embarrassing, and I wished that I could go home to my parents, who both sang in tune.

I don't know if my mother paid for us to go to the cinema one Saturday afternoon, I expect she did. Flo knew where to go, and without any reference as to what was showing or what time the film began, two tickets were bought and we were ushered, in near darkness, into two front seats. I thought we were near enough to touch the screen. I could only see the whole picture by lifting my head backwards as far as it would go. It was a film, I remember, in black and white, where two men were having a heated conversation in a lighthouse.

Before I could begin to understand anything relating to a story, Flo gave me a nudge and signalled to go. We certainly did not have our monies' worth, but I didn't feel I was in a position to complain.

Flo was growing up, and her attention began to drift away from me. It was a timely development, as the family were planning to move again, and I was changing schools.

I was grateful for Flo's friendship. She showed me another side of life, that not everyone was as fortunate as I was, with a comfortable home and a father who was advancing in his profession and providing well for his family. Flo would be going out into the world with none of the advantages that I had. I admired her confidence. The future called to both of us, but we would go in different directions.

Chapter 3

No cul-de-sac now. We lived in a detached house in a road of detached houses, some much larger than ours. Fyle Avenue was a road I was to walk up and down twice a day for several years. I became familiar with every gateway, every garden, tree and flower throughout the seasons. I knew every irregularity in the pavement, where water collected after a shower of rain. I rarely met anyone. I was at school after the milkman's round, and before the groceries were delivered. I was home again before the office exodus.

The outlook for finding a replacement for Flo was slim; no one from my new school lived in my direction. It became a life of observation for any signs of movement, keeping my wits about me at school and making an effort to come out of my shell in this new environment. I did miss Flo.

My mother was the first of us to spot a head out of the burrow. Passing up the road one day a little while after our arrival, she halted as a lady her own age was about to step out of her front gate into mother's path, a high hedge preventing her approach. An occurrence so rare could not be passed without a friendly greeting and introduction as, despite the outward impression of privacy at all costs, news of the newcomers had been circulated. Also, it had been observed that I was a member of the household, and of an age to be company for the young daughter of my mother's new acquaintance. It transpired that we girls were the only young children in the road.

Elizabeth went to a small private school. She was a year younger than I was, even so my mother accepted an invitation for me to take tea one afternoon after school and meet her. I felt I was chosen to be a Flo to her.

As soon as I entered number nineteen, I sensed that I had walked into an entirely different world. "Were they friends of the king, that they displayed such lovely pictures?" I wondered. The elaborate ornaments on the mantlepiece spoke to me of royal connections. All was confirmed as I sat at table in the dining room, where tea was taken in such pretty cups and saucers, with matching plates for tempting cakes, arranged on a cake stand. Even my mother's best tea service was not as pretty as this.

Elizabeth's personal possessions were kept in her bedroom, and after tea I was taken upstairs to see them. I duly followed, feeling that I must be on my very best behaviour, making every effort to be as friendly as possible. Was I as delicate in Flo's eyes as Elizabeth seemed to me? On passing the hall, I glanced through an open door into another room, hoping to see if Elizabeth's parents had a piano, and to my great delight, they did. It was a baby grand! Would I ever get the chance to play it?

I was most interested in Elizabeth's collection of books, which showed that for her age she was exceedingly well-read. She had far more books than I had, and I felt at a disadvantage in discussing my preference for certain authors. My own books tended to be annuals.

Elizabeth's mother was kindness itself. She encouraged me to visit and spend time with her daughter. I recalled the day Elizabeth and I were playing in the well cared for garden, when her mother joined us, taking me around to study the flowerbeds. From her I learned the names of flowers, aquilegia, gypsophila, clematis, azalea and chrysanthemums. At home my father concentrated on growing vegetables, he was good at that.

I can't quite remember how it happened, but one day, returning to school after lunch, I called in to see Elizabeth's mother. As I was about to ring the bell, I heard her singing a song I knew. I told her that I could play it on the piano. She led me into the drawing room, I sat down at the grand piano and she found the music for me. I was in heaven; she sang and I played. The time passed so quickly that I suddenly realised I was late for afternoon school. I missed the first lesson and crept in as the girls moved from one classroom to another. My absence was never noticed.

I think Elizabeth's mother was an accomplished singer. I was unaware of any outlet for her to perform outside the home. We became close to each other as we made music together. My piano teacher at this time was very keen for me to accompany her when I told her about our friendship, and she gave me good advice in the art of accompanying. I think both my parents came to hear us one day. Elizabeth had piano lessons, but she would never play when I was in the house, nor do I think she accompanied her mother, which was sad, really.

They say all good things come to an end, but I could have wished for something kinder. Elizabeth's mother became ill, and a great sadness descended on the household. My visits had become more infrequent as Elizabeth and I grew older, each concentrating on our busy lives of study. When her mother died, she and her father moved away. Everything about my friendship with Elizabeth's mother was treasured. Music drew us together and I loved her for her interest in me, and her encouragement as I began to appreciate the subtleties of accompanying. I lost touch with her daughter.

Chapter 4

As I lived the life of a young teenager, I had no idea that I was putting down memory markers for when I became an old lady. The days passed.

I had discovered a narrow passageway between two houses, connecting my road with another road going in the same direction towards my school. I had no reason now to pass the house so frequently visited, and decided to vary my journey. In doing so, I fell in with a girl my own age. She was in a different stream at school, which meant that we didn't see each other once inside the building. I liked that, because we couldn't talk or gossip about other girls with whom we both came into contact.

I looked out for Sheila, waiting for her if I spotted her in the distance, as she had further to walk than I did.

It soon became obvious that Sheila's passion in life was horse riding. She informed me that she cycled several miles into the country on Saturday mornings to ride when she had saved sufficient pocket money. I had never thought of doing such a thing. However, with a little encouragement, I agreed to accompany her when I too had sufficient money for a lesson and, importantly, permission from my mother to go with her.

There was still war between our country and Germany at this time, but it was peaceful where we lived, and a cycle ride through the countryside to the stables was not really a problem.

As a beginner, I was not allowed to jump on a horse and gallop off willy-nilly. My chosen mount, a docile animal, was attached to the instructor's horse by a leading rein, and it walked dutifully as a group of us set off on well-worn paths. Sheila was free to canter off ahead with the more advanced riders.

My pleasure, given the sedate pace in which we proceeded, was in being seated high up, looking over hedges and feeling superior. Superior to what I couldn't actually say, the feeling was there, nevertheless. They were very enjoyable hours. I did learn to trot, but that was as far as my horsemanship went. During the holidays when we couldn't go to the stables, we planned to go off cycling.

Before the war started, as a family, my father drove us out into the countryside at the weekends to picnic. I became familiar with the route he took to a favourite spot high up overlooking woods and farmland. In the distance we could see the sea on a clear day; or thought we could.

It followed therefore, that when the question arose as to where we should go for our cycle ride, I suggested the same spot, saying I knew the way very well. We set off with a clear goal in sight and a determination to reach it. The morning was fine, so it was assumed the whole day would be fine. I did so want the trip to be a success; Sheila was putting her trust in me as I had done when we cycled to the stables on my first outing with her.

The distance covered by our car to reach the chosen look-out, didn't seem as long as the distance we were cycling to get to it. There were more hills than I remembered, and long stretches of road that seemed to go on for ever. Finally, we reached the top of a hill where a small car park overlooked the beautiful view. We had arrived.

Rest and a sandwich revived us, and we sat, elated that our effort had given us such a reward. Similar, we thought, to that which climbers must feel when they reached the summit of a mountain. We had to climb, and on occasions get off our bikes and push. At least our way back would be easier, we had thought, as we turned for home. It was just as well it was, for the dark clouds we noticed in the distance as we sat admiring the sun-drenched valley at our feet, soon caught up with us. However hard we peddled, we could not escape the heavy drops of rain and inevitable downpour, which kept company with us on our way. Sheila arrived home before I did. She gave me a cheery goodbye and said it had been fun, even though she must have been soaked to the skin. I had another half mile to ride before I pushed my bike into the garage and opened the back door.

"You're wet," said my mother.

"I was drenched," said Sheila, when we met up again. She was a good sport.

On another occasion we cycled to a small seaside resort along the coast, and took our swimming costumes. We couldn't swim at home as our beach was off limits. I don't know why this little beach was open, maybe the high cliffs protected it from invasion. Sheila was a good swimmer, whereas I couldn't swim at all well. I bounced up and down with the mass of youngsters a few yards from the beach, fearful that I would get knocked over. Sheila on the other hand, swam out well beyond the dippers. She joined me after a while, panting and grinning, clearly having enjoyed herself. She made no comment about my poor effort, keeping my feet firmly on the bottom most of the time. I did enjoy being in the water up to a point and she was good company.

I didn't want Sheila to move away. Just as I had moved from the north of the country to the south, so Sheila's family were moving from the south coast to the north of England. Ours was a very private friendship; I was never invited to Sheila's home, nor did I ever invite her to mine. It seems most unsociable now. I don't know why that should have been. Almost overnight Sheila moved out of my life. I can't even remember saying good bye to her. I suppose I was getting used to the comings and goings of people I met briefly. Nevertheless, we didn't keep in touch. We were both going on to further our education, and we had enough to think about without writing letters.

With the war over, peacetime brought about its survival problems as we entered into the rhythm of normal daily life again.

Chapter 5

I moved on. I had begun my career, putting into practice all I had learnt at college, finding daily, that my education was continuing as both teacher and pupil.

It was imperative that I should find somewhere to live in North London where I intended staying for the foreseeable future. Somewhere not too close to my place of work, but conveniently near public transport and the shops.

Studying away from home had been an introduction into sharing amenities, but I looked for more independence if that was at all possible. My salary, at two hundred and fifty pounds a year, precluded any luxurious accommodation. I needed a room of my own where I could make a meal and have the use of a bathroom.

Before I began my first day at work, I travelled up to spend a day looking for a bedsit within my means. I had seen advertisements in our local newsagents at home, offering rooms to let, so I did have some idea as to what to look for. The variation in price asked tended to be a pointer to the comfort one could expect.

So, without hesitation, on my arrival I made for the local newsagents, to buy a paper and at the same time to study the advertisements in the window for accommodation. One advertisement, neatly written on a postcard, caught my attention before I opened the paper. Mrs Dean at seven de Prinz Road was offering a bedsit to a single professional lady at a modest rent. I looked at my map of the area, and found the road in question within easy reach of a bus stop, which would take me close to my place of work. Could that be worth a visit, and would I have the courage to turn it down if it proved unsuitable? Number seven was supposed to be a lucky number, there would be an element of luck in finding a place which was perfect for all my needs.

No wonder my parents were not taken in by my forced bravado, when I told them of my plans. Of course, they were pleased that my application to join the staff of a school requiring a pianist, was accepted, but they would have liked me to have settled nearer home, where they could keep an eye on me. My choosing to go to London had filled them with misgiving. At the time, I didn't appreciate their concern, I was very persuasive, and assured them that I could manage on my own. The thought of the concerts that I could attend was like a magnet to me.

I was nervous at opening the paper standing outside the newsagents — I couldn't see a café in which to hide myself away to study it. I made up my mind to walk to de Prinz Road and see what kind of a house number seven was before I knocked on any other door. My map allowed me to take a short cut, away from the main road and bus route. I soon found myself walking down quiet roads of identical Victorian houses. I turned a corner into the road I was aiming for. The houses were semi-detached, with small insignificant front gardens, but imposing front doors. Number seven looked well kept, and without a second thought I knocked gently, twice, and waited a while, beginning to think there was no one in, but eventually the door opened.

A middle-aged lady gave a cheerful, "Hello," and I enquired about the room I had seen advertised.

"Come in, and I will show it to you," she said, opening the door wider. "I'm Mrs Dean."

I thanked her and introduced myself, following her into the hall, which had an old-fashioned air about it. It struck me as being clean and having no unpleasant stale smell of cooking. "A good sign," I thought.

"The room is upstairs," she continued. "Have you come far?"

I followed her as she climbed the stairs, and answered that I had come up from the coast for the day, and was shortly beginning work nearby, and I was looking for accommodation.

We reached the first floor where I had expected to stop, but along the landing I could see another flight of stairs to which Mrs Dean was leading me. We continued up to a small landing where two closed bedroom doors confronted us.

"The accommodation is in the back room overlooking the garden," Mrs Dean explained, as she opened the door into an attic room.

It was surprisingly light with the sun streaming through a window set in the slope of the roof. It was a fair size. I noticed a hand basin on the wall a few feet from the door. On the opposite wall there was a fireplace containing a gas fire. The furnishings were adequate for one not used to a luxurious bedroom at home; the room was carpeted in a rather gaudy pattern, but appeared fairly new. There was a single bed under the eaves, a small table, rather like the old card table we had at home, an arm chair and a huge old fashioned wardrobe. There was a cupboard next to the hand basin for storing food, with an electric ring on top.

I glanced out of the window, there wasn't a great deal to be seen as I was so high up. There was a better view of the gardens to the rear of the property.

"The bathroom is on the first floor," explained Mrs Dean, "and is shared by two other lady tenants.

I will show you on the way down. There are a few house rules, naturally," she continued in a voice that betrayed an educated background. "The house is locked at ten thirty, unless you inform me beforehand that you intend to be coming back later. We respect each other's privacy and do not indulge in loud music. Ladies may decide amongst themselves when the bathroom is free for baths, just two baths are allowed in one week. Rent is always paid in advance."

She said this in the same way that I remembered the headmistress at school speaking to us when I was young. She who must be obeyed. It was not said unkindly, I expect she had repeated these words several times as people had come and gone. There was probably a reluctance on her part to take in lodgers, sharing her home with strangers.

I couldn't think of a reason to turn away from accepting to rent the room, I really had no desire to return to the newsagents and start again. One could always move on. The agreement was made that I should take up residence at the beginning of the following week. It would give me time to settle in before starting work in earnest.

I returned home to explain to my parents that I would be leaving the family home, and taking up residence at seven de Prinz Road in a week's time. I described how near it was to my place of work, to shops and public transport. They were concerned, but I promised that I would telephone home every week and, of course, come home at the end of the school term. I felt confident and excited at becoming independent and earning a salary. They must come and visit me, I said. It is only now, as I look back over so many years, that I can appreciate what a wrench it was for my parents when the time came for me to leave the nest. I am thankful that they had each other for support.

Chapter 6

I took the underground from Waterloo to the local tube station and, because my case was heavy, I caught the bus to the end of de Prinz Road.

Mrs Dean was expecting my arrival, and greeted me pleasantly, there was a motherly note in her voice which I found very reassuring. Even so, I was given keys for my room and the front door, and left to carry my case, various bags and my handbag, upstairs by myself. After the noise of traffic, the house was absolutely quiet. I supposed the other tenants were at work.

There was no sun this time to shine into my attic room and coming in from the daylight outside, the room struck me as being rather dark. There was a small improvement when I turned on the main electric light; the bedside lamp was brighter, and cheered me as it was quite adequate for reading. I dismissed the wish that the room could have been lighter, and set about opening my suitcase and hanging my few clothes in the oversized wardrobe. It didn't take long for me to place my personal effects on the small shelf at the side of the fireplace, and my alarm clock on the bedside table. I had taken possession.

Having sorted out my personal belongings, I freshened up and set off for my first foray to the high street shops, list in hand, to buy the essentials. Once the week was over and the term proper began, I was assured of a good cooked mid-day meal at school every day. My parents had given me money, a kind of float, to purchase food and any other necessities until my first cheque arrived. I was grateful to them. I sincerely hope I was, looking back, as they had to pay for my lodgings in advance. I intended to repay them, and I hope I did, but I have no recollection of doing so, it was a long time ago now.

On returning, Mrs Dean met me in the hall. "I'll take you up to see Miss Parker in the back room, she will explain to you the use of the bathroom. She is my long term resident, so I expect my new residents to fit in with her," she explained. I thanked her and followed her up the stairs to the landing on the first floor. She knocked on a door, opening it as she did so, announcing her presence.

"Hello, Peg," she said, "I've brought Miss Pitters to see you, she is our new resident."

I left my shopping on the landing and followed my landlady into the room. Turning to me she said, "I've told Miss Parker all about you joining us, so I will leave you both to sort out your bathroom times." She then left the room, closing the door quietly behind her.

I was not good at judging the ages of ladies much older than myself, but I guessed that Miss Parker was about the same age as my mother. She turned in her chair, which was facing the window overlooking the back garden.

"Come and sit down and let us introduce ourselves." There was a slight lilt in her voice which suggested that she came originally from Scotland. "Do call me Peg," she continued.

I moved forward to a seat that was next to hers. Her room was identical in size to my own which was directly above it, although it seemed larger as there was no slanting ceiling.

"Hello," I said, "I am Susan. I understand I share the bathroom with you."

Without more ado she said, "I am not as young as I was, I am retired now. I used to work in Henderson's in the High Street, in the office. Unfortunately, I suffer from arthritis in my knees and I can't walk very well. My sister comes twice a week to help me in the bathroom. If at any time she can't manage to come, we have to alter the date. Monday and Thursday evenings are her usual times for coming. Could you just check though, to see if the bathroom is free on your chosen nights?" She continued, "The person who rents the front room next to yours, swims at the local baths regularly, and doesn't use our bathroom, which is very helpful."

It appeared that Peg seldom left her room. It was painful for her to climb up and down the stairs unaided. Her restricted world consisted of her radio, her newspaper — which Mrs Dean took up for her each day with her milk — and her books, which her sister brought her from the library. She assured me she had visitors, friends with whom she worked at Henderson's.

I enquired as to how she managed with shopping. "Ah," she explained, "the grocers next door to Henderson's, where I have been a customer for many years, delivers my order each week. Mrs Dean prepares a lovely Sunday roast for me, and I can manage simple meals on my stove. My sister is a great help too. So far, so good," she added with a smile. A bit embarrassed at her non-stop revelations, I excused myself saying that I was keen to put my shopping away and settle in.

On returning to my room I was very conscious of the fact that Peg was right underneath, and that she wouldn't be happy to hear heavy movements overhead. I had no radio at the moment, but I did intend buying one, so that I could listen to plays and concerts. I was very aware that I would have to keep the volume down to avoid any complaint. The house was so quiet, if anyone was listening to a radio, I could not hear it.

I looked forward to meeting the resident from the front bedroom. It must be someone young if they visited the local baths, I thought.

Chapter 7

I had several meetings before starting the term proper, and I felt more relaxed as the day came for me to put my timetable into practice. There were other members of staff who were also new, and I found it easy to enter into congenial conversation.

My rising each morning, getting my breakfast and leaving my room in time to catch the bus, became routine. The house was always very quiet as I closed the front door. Once I thought I could just detect the sound from a radio coming from Mrs Dean's rooms on the ground floor, but it was very faint, and I couldn't linger to pay attention to it.

I had met my neighbour next door, if you could call it a meeting. When we were within sight of each other, in the hall or on the stairs, there was a quick subdued, "Hello," a hurrying on to some appointment or other, or an eagerness to reach her room and close the door.

Maybe people had come and gone with such regularity, she didn't see the need to get to know me. Not one to intrude on another's privacy, I responded in like manner in as friendly a way as possible. I didn't dare enter into conversation, being the younger and a newcomer. I recalled Mrs Dean's instructions that privacy was observed. I was very much in the adult world and would have to tread with care.

I returned late after school one day, when the evenings were pulling in earlier and earlier, Peg was standing outside her door, stick in hand. "Hello Susan," she greeted, and without waiting for a greeting from me, she said, "I wonder if I could ask you to post a letter for me?"

"Yes, of course I can, Peg." I readily agreed, as I knew the post-box was quite nearby.

"Come inside while I look for a stamp," she said, leading the way into her room.

The hallway and stairs were never very warm and Peg's room seemed invitingly cosy. "Do sit down." she said.

I sat in the armchair by the window, putting my school bag and handbag on the floor beside me. Peg took a while looking for a stamp, her letter in her hand.

"You look as if you could do with a cup of tea," she said, "I'll put the kettle on."

I really did not want to stop, I was anxious to reach my room, but her kettle was on the ring and her cups and teapot on a tray ready. I found myself saying how kind she was, and that a cup of tea was always welcome.

It was a good hour before I was able to leave politely. The conversation had been nearly all one way as I answered questions about my home, my parents, my college life, and my piano playing. I was disconcerted by her probing, although I was sure it was a polite enquiry. Even so, I did not enjoy divulging so much information about my family and background. I was glad to reach my room where I placed her letter in my handbag, to be posted on my way to work. I glanced at the address and noticed it was meant for a married person living in Scotland, a friend perhaps.

I had been hoping that when I had settled in at school I would be able to find a member of staff to accompany me to a concert or to the theatre one Saturday evening, but I hadn't been able to broach the subject. Staff members seemed to be either married or engaged to be married and were not seeking friendship outside school. I was not too concerned, and did venture out to concerts, but after a while, not having company somehow made the outings less pleasurable. When the lights were down and the music began, it made no difference whether or not I had a companion. However, during the intervals and on the journey home, I felt an uncomfortable loneliness.

Peg was standing outside her door when I returned one afternoon towards the end of my first year. I thought she wanted me to post another letter for her, I had done so several times, stopping for a cup of tea on occasions. I was aware that she looked forward to my company for a while. This time however, she invited me into her room after I had finished my supper, to listen to a concert being broadcast from the Royal Albert Hall. A well-known pianist was playing a Beethoven piano concerto. As yet I had not bought a radio of my own. I was often required to work after school playing for concerts and that required my staying for rehearsals. I would come back and read.

Peg's invitation came unexpectedly, and I eagerly accepted. She was never so inquisitive after that first afternoon when I had tea with her; she would tell me of places she had visited abroad in her younger days. She told me about her family and related stories of holidays, when she and her younger sister, accompanied by their aunt, uncle and cousins, stayed at seaside resorts on the west coast of Scotland before the war. "Great family reunions they were," she said.

I suppose I was a good listener. After teaching and using my voice all day, it was quite a pleasure for me to sit and listen to someone else who had an interesting tale to tell. There was nothing about Peg's person which stood out, I had decided, as I sat with her on numerous occasions. Her hair was at that in-between stage, neither brown nor grey, and just short and straight. I guessed her sister cut it for her. She wore hardly fashionable glasses, she was inclined to be "dumpy", as my mother would say, and because she often experienced pain in her knees, her expressions alternated between a grimace and a smile.

In the quietness of her room with neither of us speaking, we listened that evening to the concert from the Royal Albert Hall – Beethoven's fourth piano concerto, played with such clarity and feeling. Peg was a good listener and did not interrupt the performance by starting to talk. I could never understand how folk could talk and listen at the same time. At the end of the first movement, when we could hear a sound of people shifting in their seats and the odd irrepressible cough, Peg just looked across at me and smiled. It said all that was needed to express admiration.

At the end of the performance, I thanked Peg and stood up to go. I had things I wanted to do before bed. We had become relaxed in each other's company and, although she would have liked me to stay longer, I knew she would be content that we had listened to the Beethoven together. I was grateful for her company, she was the only one who kept loneliness at bay in my first year working away from home. I think had she been mobile, we would have enjoyed going to concerts together.

It didn't take me long to realise I was not satisfied with my attic room. During the winter months when the sun had moved so as not to shine through my window at any time during the day, the weekends were rather dismal for me. I always planned to visit an art gallery or museum, but often I came back to a cold drab room to heat up something for my supper. I missed my piano more than I realised, although an instrument was always available at school.

I was still young and I needed more company. I had not acquired a radio. I think at the back of my mind quite early in my tenancy, I decided my stay at seven de Prinz Road would be temporary.

I began to search for more comfortable accommodation. I made a point of getting to know the district nearer to my work. My first experience of a landlady in Mrs Dean, made me wish for someone a little more friendly. I hardly saw her; my rent was put in an envelope and placed through a slit in a box on the hall stand each week. Now and then, I would meet her coming out of Peg's room at the weekend. "Was it a social visit, or had she gone to collect the rent?" I wondered. Peg never spoke about her, apart from saying that she was grateful for her Sunday lunch. I saw Peg's sister coming and going, but she never stopped to talk.

I found that I wasn't at all emotional saying good-bye when the time came for me to move on. I was sorry for Peg, more than anything. She would be on the lookout for someone else to post her letters. I hoped that she found a person of her own age to keep her company sometimes, although I doubted if anyone but a youngster, pushed to find a roof over their head, would contemplate staying in the attic room for long.

There was a very formal handing over of my keys to Mrs Dean. I guessed that the card advertising a room to let would soon be on view in the newsagents near the underground station.

Chapter 8

Sometimes the unforeseen can be to one's advantage. I found I had no need to be concerned financially when looking for new accommodation. My father's unmarried sister had recently died and left me a legacy, just at the time I was seriously searching for somewhere else to live.

My parents felt they had to step in with advice, and after my first attempt resulting in de Prinz Road, I was only too willing to be guided through the intricacies of renting a small furnished property. I succeeded in finding a flat over a shop in the busy area a stone's throw from my school. It was ideal for me; not large, with a small kitchen, a bathroom and a bedroom at the rear and a large living room in the front overlooking the road. A flight of steps to the side of the building led to a long balcony which traversed the back of several shops, each with a flat and its front door. I saw signs of relief on the faces of my parents as they saw me settle in comfortably before they returned to the south coast.

There was plenty to do in the flat before I could really feel at home, but a pot plant or two, a pottery jug and Bach and Beethoven did wonders to make up for the lack of pictures on the walls.

It didn't take long for me to establish a routine for practise. I rose in time to arrive at school an hour before my teaching began. Even in the dark mornings, I was not reluctant to get out of bed. There were plenty of people about at an early hour. It began to be quite normal for me. I could always make myself a cup of tea in the staff room after playing. Sometimes I stayed late in the practise room, learning new works purely for my own pleasure. The school itself was not closed — evening classes took place after the children had gone home.

As I was packing away my music one evening, there was a gentle tap on the door. Looking up I could see a lady through the glass window and I signalled for her to come in.

She explained that she was looking for an accompanist for a local mixed choir to which she belonged. She had heard me in passing along the corridors, and wondered if I would be interested in playing for them. I understood their present accompanist was retiring and, as choir secretary, she was searching for a replacement.

My heart almost missed a beat. I asked for her details as to the kind of music the choir sang, and of concerts in the pipe line. I knew I would be auditioned, but jumped at the chance. I realised I had been in the right place at the right time. Then and there I accepted an invitation to attend the choir's next rehearsal, meet the outgoing accompanist, and most importantly, the choir's conductor.

The following week, without any prior preparation, I found myself playing for a large choir, as they rehearsed in the hall of another local school, preparing for their next concert. All went well; the conductor had a clear beat, and the choir had been well trained.

I began to know secretary Philippa Strange quite well in the weeks which followed, for my appointment was made official.

My contact with the choir's conductor was pleasant and professional; for what I called the office side of my work with them, my contact was with Philippa. I was so pleased to be able to invite her to my flat to hear more of the concerts the choir had performed in the past, and the charities they had supported and to discuss the music chosen for the rest of the year. None of the choir members was a professional singer, each gave of their ability for the joy of singing together.

I looked forward to rehearsal nights and the warm welcome I was given every time I arrived. It was a complete change from the work I did at school. I relished the opportunity to study new choral works. The performances, geared mainly around the Christian festivals of Christmas and Easter, were dated before the actual festivals, which meant that I was free to return home for the holiday, to relax with my parents and recharge my batteries. I was the practise pianist, and on the nights of the public performances a good supportive orchestra accompanied the singers. I was always present for the concerts. When occasionally the choir sang secular songs, I played the piano for that performance.

Although Philippa was a few years older than I was, we enjoyed each other's company. She was married and had a young son who, following in his father's footsteps, was away at boarding school. It seemed inevitable that, after several visits to my flat to discuss choir matters, I was invited to supper to meet her husband.

By now, I was growing in confidence and felt at ease among colleagues at work. My parents had encouraged me to be myself, neither giving myself airs or belittling myself in a bashful pose. I was quite relaxed going to supper with Philippa and her husband. Suitably dressed, with a small box of liqueur chocolates, I arrived promptly on the appointed evening.

The home where Philippa lived was very like the house in de Prinz Road. There was no need to rent rooms here. I had only ever been a guest in what I called a posh house once before, and that was where Elizabeth's parents had lived back home. A single step over the threshold, and I was in a different world of elegance. What on earth did Philippa think of my flat? But there she was, giving me a welcoming hug and drooling over the proffered chocolates.

"Come through, Susan, and meet William. We are having a drink before supper. Will you join us?" she asked.

I had not met many men in my life; I attended a single sex school and studied at an all ladies' college. The men at work were older than I was, and were busy in their teaching, coming and going, always seemingly in a hurry, tweedy sort of men, with the smell of cigarette or pipe wafting in the air, as they passed.

Agreeing to join her and her husband in a pre-supper drink, I followed Philippa into their sitting room. William came towards me, hand outstretched. (I remember this moment so well.) He was tall, well built, dressed in a dark pinstriped suit; he possessed a mop of grey hair and had fine features. He was a very handsome man. I just had enough strength of voice to ask for a dry sherry, with thanks, and became shyness itself.

Philippa began taking charge as we sat with our drinks, and it wasn't long before the conversation led to questions about my parents and my home on the south coast. "The ice breakers again," I thought, though grateful to be launching out on a subject I knew something about. I, in turn, asked after their son, Christopher. They were both eager to show me photographs of him, saying how well he'd settled at school, but that they were looking forward to having him home for the coming holiday.

Supper was a most enjoyable meal for me, far more elaborate than my usual Friday night fish and chips. I was still nervous at meeting William's gaze, and it was a relief to follow Philippa into the kitchen to clear away the dishes after we had finished. Our conversation there was more relaxed. She told me that her husband worked in a bank in the city. He had served in the Forces during the war, and had been a prisoner of war for over a year. She explained that he liked to lead a quiet life.

After coffee, I indicated to Philippa that I ought to be heading for home. William thanked me for coming, and hoped that I would come again as they had both enjoyed my company. Philippa wouldn't hear of my going home by bus, so I was driven all the way back in style.

Once in my flat, I thought how fortunate I was to know them both; what a lovely home they had, and how warm they had been towards me. I put it down to the fact that I accompanied the choir, but then, that need not have led to the friendship between us. My life seemed secure with my position at school, my interest in playing for the choir, and my friendship with Philippa and her husband.

Chapter 9

In the centre of town, quite close to my flat, a few yards down the road, there was a large open car park. It was used during the day by office workers and shoppers, but at night local residents left their cars there, ready to transport them to their place of work in the morning.

When my parents accepted an invitation to come and stay at the flat for a few days, the fact that my father could leave his car safely nearby was an encouragement for them to drive up, a much better option for them, as they would be free to explore the outlying countryside and small towns close to North London.

My bedroom possessed a double bed, and my front room had a large sofa, so there was no problem regarding sleeping accommodation. Fortunately both my parents were very mobile, and the steps up to the balcony were negotiated without comment.

They had heard of my friendship with Philippa and her husband, and how I came to meet them. At my mother's suggestion, I invited them to join us for supper at a local restaurant, which had a good reputation. I was pleased at the opportunity to repay them for their kindness to me, and for them to have the chance to meet my folks.

I was proud of my parents. My father, nearing retirement, had risen in the civil service to a post of responsibility. My mother had been involved in voluntary work from as far back as I could remember; in their way, both had contributed to the war effort, now thankfully at an end.

On the evening arranged for our meeting, father drove us to the restaurant. I knew my friends would arrive on time, eager to meet my family. Philippa would have no difficulty conversing with my parents, but I was concerned for William, who often sat quietly listening to us when I visited. He was always charming towards me, but I confess, I was a bit in awe of him, a feeling of being in front of the headmaster. Silly, really.

I need not have worried, as he appeared very relaxed, ready to enjoy the evening with its promise of good food and wine. Nothing disappointed. As I ate my meal I was pleased at the ease with which my four guests interacted. I found myself listening and joining in when I could. Philippa and William spoke of where they had been brought up, and that was of interest to me.

When the meal was over, I attempted to pay for it, but my father intervened and settled the account. William helped Philippa on with her coat in a gentlemanly fashion, as did my father assisting my mother. How right it seemed, I thought, this pairing, as I struggled with my coat until William came to my aid.

We said our farewells with thanks all round. It had been a successful evening. I was pleased to be going back to the flat with my parents for company. The evening, though, had highlighted the fact that I had no man to help me on with my coat, to take my arm and lead me out of the restaurant, help me into the car. I had not felt this lack of a male escort so strongly before. Philippa and I had been to plays together in London, when two tickets had been bought and William had decided not to go, knowing that I would be only too pleased to accept a free seat. Philippa was such good company and I believe she enjoyed being with me.

She never complained about her husband. Realising his war experiences had had an effect on him, it was a subject that was never discussed. She accepted his decisions to stay home quietly sometimes. But this evening, I surprised myself by an inward longing to meet a member of the opposite sex, and fall in love.

Life returned to normal after my parents returned home; normal that is, in that my usual routine of teaching, accompanying, and occasional visits into the world of entertainment continued. I calmly told myself there was no urgency, but I would keep my eyes open for Mister Right and acknowledge my desire for loving companionship. A few weeks later, Philippa asked me to stay behind after choir, as she had something to tell me. She and William had returned from a long holiday with Christopher at their cottage on the east coast to discover that she was pregnant, expecting a child, early the following year. Of course, I was delighted for her, and the family. I felt not a little envious, I must confess. Philippa insisted that I would be an honorary aunt to both children from now on, and would be welcome at any time.

Chapter 10

Looking back over the years, I wouldn't have deemed it possible for a small, unintended, careless act on my part, to change my life completely, but it did, and it had nothing to do with Philippa.

Collecting my music case and handbag after school one afternoon, preparing to leave work, in fumbling to assign which load to which hand, I dropped my handbag. It was open, and the contents fell out on the floor. I wasn't in haste, and bent down to gather up the oddments that every woman carries around. I left to walk home. I climbed the steps to my flat. I was tired, and a cup of tea would be most welcome. I put my hand in my handbag for my key, but it wasn't there.

There aren't many worse feelings one can have, then to arrive home tired, and be unable to get in. Outside, desperately wanting to be inside, refusing to realise that without the key, the door will remain shut. How could I end up finding myself in this situation; I felt like dissolving into tears of frustration.

Taking a deep breath, pulling myself together, I considered my options. I could return to school and look for my key, which I was sure would be there, hidden out of sight on the floor, or, before hastening back, I could look to see if it was possible to prise open the bathroom window, and gain access that way. The window was certainly wide enough, I just needed some sort of tool.

As I was pondering what to do, a young man came up the steps, stopped, seeing my bags deposited outside my front door, and me closely examining my bathroom window, guessed that I had locked myself out.

"Ah," he said, "locked yourself out?"

"Yes," I replied in the affirmative, still on the verge of tears.

"Do you want me to help?"

"Please," I said, too emotional to say more.

"We will have to take off the metal grill on the window, then you can put your arm through and lift the latch. I'll go and fetch my screwdriver, and we will see what we can do."

With that, he disappeared into his flat further along the balcony.

I studied the window, and saw the possibility of what he had suggested, the removal of the ventilation grill was something I had not considered. I didn't have long to wait. He returned, and set about lifting the lead flashing to release the grill without damage. I reached up, putting my bare arm through the opening. I couldn't stretch down far enough. Despairingly, I withdrew it.

"I can't reach," I moaned.

"I'll give you a lift up," he said, and when I had collected myself, I let him lift me bodily, enough for me to release the arm of the latch. In a second the window was open. I gasped with sheer delight.

"I'll see you in," he said, and without more ado, he again lifted me bodily as I carefully climbed, head first, on to the top of the toilet seat, reaching for the side of the hand basin to steady myself. With the man guiding my feet, I bent my knees enough to swivel my body through in an ungainly fashion, everything showing which shouldn't, but I was home.

I opened my front door to find him replacing the grill.

"Don't forget to close your window," he said, "and try not to lock yourself out too many times or else the grill will be bent and won't go back properly." He continued the lesson, "Have you got a spare key?"

I assured him I had, though much good it did me left in a drawer in the flat. At the moment at least I could go to school the next day knowing I would be able to get in when I returned home.

In offering my grateful thanks, I was able to study who my knight in shining armour might be; older than I had thought, not tall, but sturdy, his friendly face grinning from ear to ear, revelling in my predicament, obviously delighted to have been of assistance.

"I am Susan Pitters," I said, offering my hand.

"Ray Benderdale," he replied, accepting it in a warm firm grip.

"Are you anything to do with Benderdales the printers?" I asked. Benderdales had premises off the High Street — they printed posters for our concerts. Philippa had often mentioned them as she was responsible for passing on information to them and picking up the posters for displaying in town.

"It's my father's firm, and I have been taken into the business. Actually, my grandfather started it in the twenties," he replied.

"Oh," I said, genuinely showing interest. "Would you like a cup of tea?" I continued in Peg-like fashion. "I am going to put the kettle on."

He accepted, and followed me into the kitchen in a relaxed friendly manner, watching me as I reached for two mugs and the tea pot. I filled the kettle.

"You've got a dripping tap," he remarked.

"Yes," I said, "I don't like to bother the landlord about it, I must get someone in to do it."

As soon as the words were out of my mouth, I knew what his reply would be.

"I'll do that for you," he said, realising I lived alone. I laughed, almost hysterically, relief at getting in and at his unexpected presence and offer.

"This is my lucky day," I said.

He came the following Saturday with a new washer, and fixed the tap. I can sit quietly now, years later, and relive every moment of this time.

Chapter 11

"You know, mother never expected Ray to marry." This was almost the first thing his sister said to me when we announced our engagement.

There was a family gathering at Ray's home for me to meet his mother and father, Vi and Alfred Benderdale, his married sister, Daphne, and her husband, Len. My own parents were delighted when we went down to the coast to tell them. Father remarked that in Ray I had a safe and steady man. I knew that.

Right from the beginning of our relationship, Ray had explained the reason he left the family home and moved into his flat. He had felt he needed his independence and a break from the past. I understood his mother had been very disappointed when his first girl friend had married someone else a few years ago. His mother had been very fond of her, as the family had known her from childhood. Vi Benderdale was looking forward to having her as a daughter-in-law, one she approved of. She thought her son would never recover from his disappointment. The result was that he was smothered by her concern and protectiveness.

Ray had the printing business to occupy his days, his golf to fill his free time; he had moved on.

After we married, we moved into the flat over the business. Latterly, I had left mine and moved in with Ray. Our new home had two bedrooms, a reasonable kitchen-diner and a large lounge; toilet and bathroom were still combined. Situated in a back street, there was no view and comparatively little sun to be seen. Ray's parents lived there in the early days of their marriage, but when they moved into a house of their own, it had remained empty, a sort of store.

It needed redecorating and renovating before we could consider it habitable, and we both spent every free hour working to bring it up to standard. In a few weeks we transformed a shabby, dark dwelling into a bright, colourful home, furnished in the modern style. Pride came out of our ears, we were so happy.

Moving in called for a celebration. When I had sufficient confidence in using the new cooker, we invited Ray's family for supper. I was still teaching and accompanying the choir, but I was determined to cook a lovely meal for this, my first effort at entertaining.

Ray's dad was what I call a background man, he left the women to talk amongst themselves, standing quietly and contentedly smoking his pipe, chatting to Len and Ray about sport. In his late fifties, with a little more weight than he should have, he had the bearing of a successful businessman. Ray was like him in looks. I took to Alfred with his kind face, never too engrossed in conversation to glance at me with an approving smile now and then.

Vi, on the other hand, made me nervous, very precise in speech and features, and correct in dress. I did so want to make a good impression. Right from the moment I met her I felt I was on probation. Knowing Ray's history, I appreciated his mother's concern for him, but I had the feeling that she had made up her mind for Ray to remain unmarried, and hers for good. Vi must have been upset when Ray moved into his flat, and now he seemed to be drifting even further away from her.

Daphne and Len I found very welcoming, no doubt pleased to have another couple in the family. Daphne said she enjoyed all my dishes, grateful to have someone cook a meal for her, I expect.

Eventually the family departed. I was so tired I could hardly keep my eyes open as we drank our coffee. Vi said it had been a lovely evening. Praise indeed.

"Saturday tomorrow," said Ray, as he gave me a kiss and a hug. "Leave the dishes." I hated doing it, but I put them to soak.

Chapter 12

Philippa had known Ray long before I arrived in North London. It was Ray whom she met at Benderdales to discuss the layout for the concert posters, and he supervised their printing. It was a complete surprise for her to hear that Ray was my chosen beau, equally for him to discover that Philippa and I were friends. Philippa was a well-spoken, well dressed lady customer he met on a professional level. Ray was a workman, dressed for managing inks and machinery, one to receive orders and take money.

Philippa and William were invited to our wedding, but their baby was due, and so they couldn't come. I had not visited Philippa as often as I would have liked, as my weekends were fully occupied preparing for our move. Some time before baby Janet was born, Philippa had retired from the choir, which meant that our only communication was by telephone. I did visit the family to see the baby, and leave a gift. I was delighted to receive an invitation to Janet's christening, an important occasion for their family.

Although I was an honorary aunt, I was not asked to be a godmother.

The loosening of our friendship was just part of the ebb and flow of life. We both had our hands full. One concert evening, when I was in the audience, Philippa was there. It was so pleasant for us to meet in the interval, and share our news.

I did not feel comfortable in asking her and her husband to supper at our home; rightly or wrongly, I felt in our back street flat it would be difficult for them to feel relaxed. I feared William would have been uncomfortable, and goodness knows what he would have had in common with Ray, he didn't play golf. "Best leave it," I thought. We couldn't afford an expensive visit to an upmarket restaurant at this time.

Ray did come to one of our concerts. He said he enjoyed it, but Saturday was his time for golf, and he came home too tired to change and set out again. Reckoned he would nod off and be an embarrassment, he said.

I was aware that music didn't play a part in his life. To be honest, I was thankful his leanings were away from the popular music of those days. That would have been difficult for me to handle. He accepted my love of classical music and was always interested in my chatter as I related our current programmes at school and with the choir. I appreciated his skill in printing, a subject he had studied at college, and in which his interest lay far beyond the everyday poster.

There were times when I felt I was not practising enough to maintain my standard, but I was so happy in my husband's company.

Chapter 13

I couldn't wait for my weekly Friday night phone call home — my news was too important.

"Hello, Mum," I said when she answered, "I'm pregnant."

She was so pleased, I heard her calling out to my dad at the top of her voice, "Susan is pregnant, isn't it wonderful!"

Serious questions followed about my health, about taking things easy, and a hundred and one other pieces of advice. Dad came to the phone, overjoyed at the thought of being a grandad. I was happy that I was able to give them news they had been waiting for ever since Ray and I were married.

It was a very precious time for us, we were neither of us youngsters, and were very moved that love had created the beginning of a new life, a child to look upon us as mum and dad, to grow up being part of us, someone whom we would love and care for all our future lives. It was a time of peaceful expectation between us. I, with a degree of nervousness, hoped that my pregnancy would be trouble free.

I had asked my parents not to contact Vi and Alfred until I had visited them with the news. Ray planned to tell his father at work on the same afternoon I was leaving school promptly and going straight to see Vi.

Normally I never knocked when I visited, I opened the back door and called out my name. On this occasion, when I was full of emotion, eager to give her my news, I realised she had a visitor. They were seated at the dining room table, a tea tray and biscuits served.

There was an awkward greeting from Vi, a slight hesitation, but there was nothing she could do but invite me to join them, and introduce her visitor.

"This is Vicky," she said to me, and to Vicky, "this is Susan."

"Hello," I said in greeting. I did know that Vicky was Ray's former girl friend. I sat down, and Vi went out for another cup and saucer. I had no intention whatsoever, of announcing my pregnancy in front of her. She sat in a sullen silence. The heavy makeup on her face accentuated her stony look. She barely greeted me.

Vi came back and poured me a cup of tea, which I took gratefully.

Without more ado, Vicky got up to go.

"I'll be off," she announced.

"Please don't go because of me," I said, eager to study the one who had rejected my husband.

"No," she insisted, "I must go, I only came by to see Vi for a minute."

Vi pushed her chair back. "I'll see you out Vicky," she said, and they both moved to the front door.

I sat sipping my tea, indulging in a biscuit. I could hear them talking quietly in the hall.

Vi returned after a fairly long interval.

"I'm sorry about that," she said. "Vicky's husband has left her for another woman."

No wonder she looked so downcast and miserable, she had come to Vi for sympathy. I didn't feel it was the right time to tell her my news. I left saying I was just passing and looked in to see her for a minute.

I called in at the printing works eager to talk to Ray and explain to Alfred about my change of plan in not telling Vi my news. It was an enormous relief to hear that Ray had been on his own all day. Alfred was away on business to do with the firm. Ray sensed that I was agitated, and drew me into his arms encouraging me to tell him the cause. So I explained. "It could all have been so upsetting for your mother, the last thing I wanted," I said.

It didn't take him long to finish printing and clear up. Upstairs in the flat, over another cup of tea, breathing a huge sigh of relief, he said, "I had a good escape where Vicky was concerned," and continued, "It is mother, who is in an awkward position, she was very fond of Vicky in the old days, but she was not enamoured with the way she behaved later on when she met Terry and married him." He paused to drink his tea. "My mum knew Vicky's mum when they were carrying us. Vicky was a bright young thing, very likeable, a bit strong willed. When her mother died unexpectedly, her dad found it difficult to manage the three children, especially Vicky, the eldest. It was then my mum tried to help; she thought of her as a possible daughter-in-law to settle both of us down. I enjoyed life with the lads then," he admitted. "I wasn't too put out when she married. Other people assumed I was, although we were never engaged."

We agreed that we would visit his parents in a day or two. I would phone Daphne directly afterwards. Vi would tell her daughter before I was able, but I was sure she would like to hear the news from me. Phoning home again was important. My mother would want to make contact with Vi to share their delight at becoming grandparents.

I remember I was beginning to realise that whereas a few years ago, my chief concern, apart from my professional life, had been for my parent's welfare, and the friend of the moment, now that I was married to Ray, I was having to think about members of his family. Although Daphne and Len had been married for a few years, they had not had any children so far. I remember having to be very sensitive of her feelings at this time. I was certain Vi and Alfred had been looking forward to their daughter giving them a grandchild, but quite definitely, my baby would be a Benderdale, bearing the family name.

Chapter 14

My probationary period was over as far as Vi was concerned. I could not have wished for more loving and attentive in-laws, eager to support Ray and me in every way possible. Philippa had been expecting my announcement for a while she said, and both she and William sent their best wishes and looked forward to the baby's arrival.

There was a fun farewell at the end of the school term. The children gave a concert in my honour. I found it very touching and shed a tear. I had been there six years — they had been happy ones. I also retired from accompanying the choir. I pushed the lack of a piano to play to the back of my mind; life was certainly changing for me.

One Saturday afternoon when Ray had gone to play golf and I was resting, book in hand but not really reading, there was a ring at the door. I rose slowly, not expecting Vi or Daphne, the only two people who came every now and then but always telephoned beforehand. I went carefully down the stairs, opened the door to find Vicky standing there.

"I've come to apologise," she said firmly. Surprised, I could only invite her in, not with the warmest of welcomes, as I was taken off guard, remembering the last time we met.

I made it a rule to tidy the lounge, which we used as a main living room, before guests came, but with no warning it wasn't looking at its best as she followed me in.

"I heard from Vi that you are expecting," she said. "I am pleased for you both."

Thanking her, I offered her a seat.

"I came to say I was sorry to leave so abruptly the other day, but I was upset and couldn't talk about it. Vi said she explained my situation, and suggested that I should make a point of apologising. So here I am."

"It was very understandable. I'm sorry it has happened," I said feeling more sympathetic and looking at her purposefully. She was the same age as Ray. The youthful looks of her twenties had passed. Despite her predilection for makeup, she was still an attractive woman and dressed smartly.

She may have guessed that Ray had told me her history. Even so, she continued to speak of her close friendship with the family and her affection for Vi.

I realised that now she found herself on her own, she would, in all probability, look to Vi for support, and lean heavily on the family.

As she showed no sign of leaving immediately, I offered her a cup of tea.

"That's very kind," she said, settling back in the chair.

I left for the kitchen, wondering how to handle the situation, I didn't want to say the wrong thing, on the other hand I must engage in conversation and say something.

As I poured the tea, emboldened by a fleeting thought of Peg, I asked her if she was contemplating divorcing her husband. She replied in a sad voice that she supposed she would, torn between wanting him to return and being angry with him for leaving her. Now he would want to be free.

"I know why he went," she confided. "He changed his mind about not wanting children. I wanted to continue my career as a fashion buyer, which is what we decided when we married."

We sat in silence. I didn't feel more questions were appropriate, and she didn't elaborate further.

After she had finished her tea, she rose to go. I thanked her for coming, and went ahead of her down the stairs to the front door.

Saying good bye, she hoped we could be friends. "Of course," I replied, and closed the door gently after her.

Returning to wash up the tea things, I found myself admiring her for coming to apologise, even at Vi's prompting, and for taking me into her confidence. Her life had not given her the security she needed. I understood from Ray that her father had married again, and her younger brother and sister had settled some distance away. It must have been marvellous for her to be courted by someone who could buy her expensive things and provide a comfortable home, but she obviously found it impossible to take motherhood on board, and had to accept the outcome.

Chapter 15

It was a great comfort for me in the later stages of my pregnancy to know that Ray was working downstairs printing. It was of concern to him when he found that both he and his father were obliged to visit the bank together on business, and only the assistant Bob would be on the premises.

Time had passed in prenatal visits to clinics and in my making clothes for the baby. I knitted a shawl, trying to occupy my fingers and my mind. I could not hide the fact that I longed to play the piano. Ray had willingly forfeited his Saturday golf on several occasions to drive me home to visit my parents for the weekend. I looked forward to going so much, I enjoyed being with my mother and father. Mum had also been busy with her knitting needles, producing matching outfits in soft colours, neither blue nor pink. I loved the fresh seaside air and relished being able to shut myself away for an hour or two, playing piano pieces long neglected.

At Ray's suggestion I planned to spend the day of their absence with Vi, and I was quite happy to do so. We were two women who loved the same man with passion, she as an adoring mother, and I as my dearest other half.

I had not made a close friend since I married, being content in Ray's company. We went out together of an evening to the cinema. On Sundays we would go for a walk around the local park. It was never so busy in those days as it became later. Sunday was always a quiet peaceful day. There was no replacement for Philippa, whom I saw very occasionally when I visited her and young toddler, Janet. She never came to the flat. I was conscious that we had no garden and very little to occupy a spirited youngster.

The day with Vi passed pleasantly, conversation was centred around her two children when they were babies. I was interested in stories of her family going back years to the time of her grandmothers. My 'he' or 'she' would have a place in her family tree, joining with that of her husband Alfred. I enquired as to whether she had written down this history, but she had no record other than an oral one and a few old photographs which I asked to see. I suggested it might be useful, now that another generation was coming along, to create a family free. "A job for you," she said.

Of course, I told her of Vicky's visit. She was pleased to hear that she had been to see me. Opening out on the subject, Vi spoke of her fondness for Vicky's mother, Margaret, whom she met when they were both expecting. Vi then explained that her own parents lived miles away in Yorkshire, travelling to see them was near impossible for her and Alfred. Her husband was attentive she said, but he was very occupied with the firm in its early days. Back then men didn't help much in the home.

I enjoyed hearing about the Benderdales. How fortunate I was to have married Ray, who was so practical in the flat, mending things that needed attention, drying dishes, and even washing up when I was feeling too tired to do it. With the family firm well established, I felt sure he would have more time for his family than his father had had when he joined the firm to assist his father in the nineteen twenties.

Ray was calling for me later in the afternoon; they both seemed very relaxed on arriving and eager to return to work, so I said my goodbyes to Vi. No doubt Ray would explain the reason for their visit to the bank when we were alone.

I had considered the problems in living at the flat after baby arrived, but I was determined to manage. The area at the foot of the stairs was large enough for a pram, that would have been my main concern had there not been room. Vi had not mentioned any difficulties when Ray was born and they lived here. But when she and Alfred recalled how inconvenient it was, they had quietly spoken to Ray. This had made him think seriously about taking out a mortgage on a house with a garden, as near the printing premises as possible. Hence, he and his father had been to seek advice on the subject at the building society in the town.

This seemed a natural progression at the time. I was delighted at the prospect, taking it for granted the legal and financial side of the move would be managed by Ray, with me on the side-lines, in a position to agree or not to agree to the choice of a future home. Life was so good.

At this time it was a little sad to receive a letter in the post informing me that Philippa and her husband had moved to the east coast, permanently. I remember sending them my best wishes. I had looked forward to inviting her and young Janet to our new home. Would we ever meet again? I wondered. I intended telling her when my baby arrived, she would be keen to know.

Chapter 16

Alice was born in due time, without fuss on my part. Both families took it in turns to declare she was the most adorable baby ever. Ray and I agreed with all their superlatives, in fact we just could not take our eyes from her. What proud parents we were, looking intently to see ourselves in her little face. I was surprised how possessive I was when others were around her.

We had many cards of congratulations. A card and gift arrived from Philippa and William. Even a school visit was requested to welcome a future pupil. And Bob at the printers, I am sure, shed a tear at seeing the new Benderdale when I showed her to him.

I didn't expect Vicky to be interested in baby Alice, but she was to the extent of giving us money to bank for her and begging to be an unofficial aunt; we could not refuse her. She continued to visit Vi, and I met her on occasion, as I often called on a Saturday when Ray was playing golf. Vicky and I would go for a walk together, she pushing Alice in her pram. I was pleased to have her company, although we had little in common. Conversation on my part was confined to the progress Alice was making and some of my family news I thought might interest her.

Now that we had moved into our small detached house, I had been able to invite my parents to stay and spend time with their grandchild. We were not fully furnished by any means, but managed with mother's help in bringing bedding. She filled my larder with enough food to stock a shop each time she came.

I was sensitive in what I felt I could talk about with Vicky, she was very much alone as regards family. I knew she had friends and had reshaped her life after her divorce and moved into a place of her own. When prompted, she was eager to talk about her recent visits to fashion shows and showrooms. She was constantly on the go, buying for a group of small individual shops. I never saw her anything other, than smartly dressed. I felt somewhat plain beside her — not that I minded. Ray would not have liked me to dress as Vicky did, her style would not have suited me at all. She was always on the lookout for new trends and fashions, which could change overnight.

Part of me was conscious of Vicky's freedom to be on the move, doing what she wanted to do. I wondered if she gave a thought to the life of love and security I enjoyed with Ray. Of course, at the back of my mind I did miss my piano. When Alice was comfortably asleep, my fingers itched to play. It wasn't that I was extremely talented in that I could make a career as a solo pianist, but I realised that to be really content within myself I had to return to playing in a serious way.

Ray was quick to say he had been waiting for me to broach the subject when I told him of my longing to return to the piano. He was very sympathetic, he needed his golf and his clubs were always ready in the cupboard under the stairs, but my piano was nowhere to be seen.

We needed a small fortune to buy everything we would have liked to furnish our home, and acquire the necessary tools for the garden which Ray was keen to tackle. There was only one income coming in and larger bills came through the letterbox.

It was decided that I would invest in a good upright piano. The family instrument, which would probably come to me eventually, was still being used by my mother. I expect when my aunt died, my parents thought the money she left would enable me to purchase a good piano of my own. I would have done so too, if I had access for it at the first flat. With my qualifications, I would be able to advertise myself as a teacher of the pianoforte, and be able to put pupils through music examinations. I daydreamed about it; it would not be long before

Alice was old enough to go to a nursery school, and I would be able to practise properly again.

I knew of a paper advertising musical instruments and gave an order for it at our local newsagents. It wasn't long before a possible instrument appeared for sale, not a great distance from where we lived, and at a price I was willing to pay. A date was made for me to inspect and play it. Vi came to sit with Alice and Ray drove me over to view it. On arrival I checked its provenance, looked carefully at the state of the action inside, and finally played pieces of some difficulty to assess the response to my touch. All in all, I agreed to the purchase, pleased that the owner had kept it well turned over the years that it had been in his possession. Ray took over the arrangements for its delivery. With handshakes all around, we left with me absolutely delighted.

There was no difficulty in deciding where it should go once home, our lounge was sparsely furnished. I just could not have been happier, I now had to wait patiently for its arrival.

Chapter 17

I had noticed that there were advertisements for pianos at reasonable prices in our local paper, even sadly, pianos given away free to anyone who could transport them. Other instruments were gaining in popularity at this time. The opportunities to play strings or woodwind were available for the young people at school — the guitar was also very popular for serious study. Pianos seemed to be too large for the smaller houses being built, and small electronic keyboards were coming onto the market, providing even more choice for the musically minded.

An advertisement as a qualified piano teacher was placed in our local paper and I waited for the telephone to ring, with a mum enquiring about lessons for their offspring. Would it be a mum wanting her child to learn, or would it be a child pestering its mother for lessons? The latter I hoped, as I had no intention of teaching a reluctant pupil.

I watched Alice with interest as she grew into a toddler, noting her reaction to the music I played especially for her — I sang to her as a baby — but I did not observe any excitement or demand for me to instruct her in how to make music herself.

It was some weeks before I received a phone call one evening from a lady member of the choir I used to accompany. She had seen my advertisement and asked if she could come and talk to me about piano lessons. A morning date was arranged. I was very hopeful that a pupil was going to materialize at last, her child would surely have some aptitude. How nice it would be to have a connection with the choir again.

Hannah arrived, and although I had not spoken to her during my days associated with the choir, I did recognise her. After pleasantries she asked if I would give her lessons, explaining that she did play the piano, but that she very much wanted to improve in order to be able to accompany her son who was making great progress on the cello. She assured me that she would be a serious pupil and practise.

I warmed to her and readily accepted her as my first student. She explained that she would only be able to come on a day which fitted in with her work at a local business. With Vi's help in looking after Alice for an hour, we were finally able to arrange a time to suit us all, and so began a most rewarding hour together. I was delighted with her progress and, because her aim was to accompany her son, I was able to help her in that direction. Before Vi left from looking after Alice, Hannah would join us for coffee and a relaxing chat about our respective families.

It was during our conversations that Hannah spoke of her son's tutor and the string quartet in which he played, and she made mention to him of her having lessons with me to improve the accompanying of her son on his cello. She said that she had also spoken to him of my past association with the choir. Opportunities for musicians to play together are never lost. I was approached, to consider joining the quartet, when a pianist was required, if my playing blended well. I went along for an audition. And so began my association with the Jones Quartet, thanks to Hannah.

As the months passed, Hannah practised faithfully, becoming more able to accompany her son when he sat for the graded cello exams. A wonderful achievement for her, as she held a part-time secretarial post, and ran her home for her husband and two children quite successfully. I doubted my ability to return to teaching at school and keep up my practise.

In the early days, when Ray and I were first married, I had helped to decorate our flat. I still enjoyed painting, brightening our home with bold colours fashionable at the time, saving on bills for redecoration. I was very occupied one way and the other, contented and fulfilled.

All too quickly, Alice was attending our local school. She was our only child, and had shown no desire to play an instrument. I accepted it. Her ability in drawing and painting was obvious and her father encouraged her in that. He took her to the printing works and she was thrilled to see the process. Her art work was displayed on parents' evening at school and Ray and I were justly proud of her. I had to accept it later on, when she took delight in the pop music of the day. Some I found enjoyable, but some I did not. I tried to show an interest in who was the rising star at a particular moment and to get used to her records being played again and again.

I treasured my mornings practising music from the classical repertoire, nevertheless. My husband and daughter had the first call on my love and attention. Both appreciated my talent. As Alice so nicely put it, "It was Mummy's thing."

Ray was justly proud when an order came in for local concert posters with my name on it.

Chapter 18

Time doesn't stand still. Alfred Benderdale had spent his life from a young age building up the family printing business. It was only natural that the time would come when he wished to retire, and he gave due notice to Ray of his intention. He might have worked longer had it not been that Vi was becoming anxious at seeing her husband coming home tired. He was not a little concerned at the development of new technologies in the printing world.

Ray had been pointing out to his father that new investment would soon have to be made now that the advancement in photocopying had hit the market, and in itself, would herald new innovations.

So there was an unsettled feeling at home as Ray tried to look into the future. I was pleased he confided in me. I had been leading a charmed life up until now with no worries, but I perceived that Ray would need all the support I could give him in the days that lay ahead.

As soon as the decision for Alfred's retirement had been conveyed officially at the business, Bob, who had worked at Benderdales almost as long as Alfred, and had been a most faithful and reliable assistant, gave in his notice of retirement. Ray had a year to decide what would be in his best interest, as he most certainly could not run the business single handed.

When he returned from work exhausted and quiet, I did my best to give him my full attention and refrained from making any demands on him relating to the house or the garden. He often became deep in thought sitting in his chair for long periods looking through magazines and books to do with printing. I let him be, making sure meals were on time. I encouraged Alice to do her homework quietly, playing her records with her ear plugs.

I had faith in Ray that he would be able to put his knowledge of printing to good use and adapt to the new technology about which he had often spoken.

It was an anxious time for the family. Daphne and Len were sympathetic, when they realised the difficulty Ray would have keeping the business going, but neither could offer any concrete ideas — they both worked in an entirely different field. However, Daphne was a Benderdale and she had a keen interest in any transactions in the pipe line.

For the moment, life continued and I felt that my small contribution to our finances — as by this time I had a few young piano pupils — was growing in importance.

But finally, Ray and his father had come to the decision to put Benderdales premises on the market. It was inevitable really; the building with the ground floor printing area, the outhouses at the rear and a good flat above, would make a very usable site for an entirely new business.

Alice had been growing up into a young lady of promise, with firm ideas as to which subject to concentrate on at school and to pursue, once she had left. It was at this time of flux that I noticed how she was drawn to Vicky. With few relatives, the smart sophisticated Vicky in the fashion world, had made a big impression on Alice, and Vicky had shown an interest in her talent in art and design. After all, Vicky had been a figure in Alice's entire life, often bringing her gifts of fashionable clothing. I never showed dislike if Alice loved what she had been given, but I must admit I would not have chosen similar things for her myself. She was growing and nothing lasted for long, I opined. She was happy and none of her parents' concerns were allowed to cause her any anxiety, although she expressed her sadness when she heard that the printing premises were to be sold.

In the course of conversation at supper one evening, I moaned about the unexpected announcement of the closure of the independent grocer where I usually shopped in the High Street. A local super-market had opened and their custom had dwindled — they could not compete. Ray had looked up with a sudden interest and asked when closure was due. I told him they had given us a month's notice. It was sad, I should miss them, as it had been a family firm for years. I immediately saw a parallel, and changed the subject.

Tired though he was, Ray finished his supper and prepared to leave, saying he was going to see his father. That puzzled me, as he had only just left Alfred after his day working with him. I naturally thought he must have forgotten something important.

I entered into conversation with Alice, promising to pay for a ticket to a local gig with her friends from school. She was a sensible lass, taking after her father, like him, wanting to spread her wings. Whereas at her age I tended to seek a friend — I remembered Sheila and the riding days — enjoying the company of a single pal, Alice loved the companionship of a small group, and a pop concert was the height of entertainment for her in her early teenage years.

Chapter 19

It had been a difficult year for Ray; the responsibility of winding down the business lay heavily on his shoulders, as in the ensuing months his father had become unwell. He was anxious for the sale of the premises to go smoothly to save his father from undue anxiety.

At the same time, Ray had been negotiating to buy the vacated grocery property in the High Street. My remark at supper one evening left him seriously thinking about transferring Benderdales to this more advantageous site. The old flatbed letterpress would be set aside, his aim was to concentrate on the new photocopying machine where he had seen an opening in the market. It wouldn't need so much space, the old grocers would be ideal.

Patience was needed all round and irritations that surfaced were soon forgotten. Eventually after what seemed a never-ending wait, news came through from the estate agent that a prospective buyer had contacted them. Baxter and Johns, a well-known local firm of carpet and flooring specialists, needed a larger area for their expanding business. Once permission had been granted to improve access into the rear of the property, there was nothing to hinder their larger vans coming through from the main road. The sale went ahead.

Vacating Benderdales was a nightmare for Ray. After so many years of unwanted bits and pieces left to gather grime, and large machinery to dispose of, it needed all his organising ability. Old Bob's grandson, looking for paid employment before going to university, joined him for a year as a valuable assistant.

The negotiations for the High Street property and the setting up of the business there, needed to go smoothly to prevent Ray's customers from going elsewhere. When Bob's grandson was preparing to leave, Ray advertised a post for a permanent assistant, able to help facilitate the opening of the new premises with the briefest closure time. New equipment had to be installed and working. It was a tense time. Ray had nailed his colours to the mast and remained cheerful despite some anxious moments.

After a week or two Benderdales was flourishing again.

Chapter 20

Ray needed a holiday — we all did. Because of Alfred's ill health, which showed no sign of improving, Ray was not keen to travel abroad, or stay away for long.

I was happy if he was able to relax, enjoy the countryside, visit the coast with its bracing sea air. I knew that he would not stop entirely from thinking about the business — wondering if his new assistant Kevin, was managing to complete the orders on time — but a different environment, good food and exercise, would do him the world of good.

Alice came with us and I encouraged Ray to bring his golf clubs and introduce the game to her. I planned to walk around a nine-hole course with them as I could not guarantee to hit the ball in a straight line and would hold up their progress, looking for balls in the long grass, if I attempted to play.

I had the feeling then that this might be the last time Alice would want to come on holiday with her mum and dad. Had she had other siblings or cousins to join us as a family, it may have been more fun for her.

As I walked around the golf course watching them, I remember becoming thoughtful about the future. Alice would leave home for further study, just as I had done. Ray would throw himself one hundred percent into the new business he was creating. There would be no more nine to five days. Looking back, I think his occasional Saturdays of golf with his friends, was a life saver at times. We all need that something else. I had my world of music, which was very precious to me and helped me feel fulfilled as a person.

Vi had realised that Alfred would not recover from his illness. I had been visiting her and helping where I could to take some of the strain from Ray. Both Daphne and Len had demanding jobs in the City, but they regularly visited Vi and Alfred at the weekends then.

Ray's sister and her husband were infrequent visitors to our home and we to theirs. We met at Vi's over the years, when they related their long holidays abroad and weekend breaks in this country, putting ideas into Alice's head — and into mine, I must admit.

To be honest, I found it difficult to equal Daphne's ring of confidence and commanding presence. I suppose it was the result of her working among people carrying responsibility, and used to making important decisions. I felt a little inadequate. I knew she was not musical, and talk of fingering a difficult passage would not interest her. Len always gravitated to Ray to talk about sport or politics. If Ray joined with the family, Len would listen attentively, but he never said much.

We did talk about our weekend breaks to the south coast to visit my parents, but at this time they were feeling their age and plans were afoot for them to move into sheltered accommodation. Even our family overnight stay with them had become too much, they just had not got the energy to entertain. Ray and I had stayed at a bed and breakfast. Sometimes Alice would come if there was no chance of an overnight stop with one of her friends whilst we were away. She had not grown up as close to my parents as she had to Vi and Alfred whom she had seen frequently. I suppose it was understandable, but they were very fond of her.

We had our memories of holidays in this country, and I still look through the albums of photographs we took. Such happy days before the business changed. We enjoyed each other's company watching Alice grow up.

A more pleasant distraction for me had been my taking driving lessons and gaining my licence, a birthday gift from Ray, although I had no car of my own at the time. To begin with there were not many opportunities for me to drive, but later I was thankful that I could.

Chapter 21

Alfred passed away. He had been moved into a nursing home where, for two years, the family had visited him regularly.

There had been a solemn funeral service in the parish church, Alfred had contributed a great deal to the community. Representatives from many businesses who were associated with Benderdales were present.

Distant relatives, friends and neighbours I had not met, attended. My parents drove up from the coast. Vicky was there, of course. It was a sad time for us all. Alfred had shown great affection for me and I loved him. Alice shed tears when he died. She was very special to him and she looked up to him as he encouraged her in her art work, supervising the printing of Christmas cards she produced for friends and family each year.

Ray grieved deeply. His father had brought him into the business, guiding him and treating him as an equal in the day to day running of the firm.

For a while Vi remained in the family home, too sad to think much about her future. She was tired and needed to rest without worry. We all kept her company when we could, and telephoned her when we could not, to see how she was coping on her own. Her main occupation had been her daily visits to see Alfred and now there was a great gap.

Vicky was like another daughter to her. She took her shopping for new clothes and made a point of going to see her. Alice went to visit her on her own and often came back to say Vicky was there.

After a while though, when the darker day came along and she found herself heating her large house with its open fires, finding it more difficult to carry in coal, clearing up the ash from the fireplace, keeping the stove in the kitchen constantly alight for her hot water, she consulted Ray about moving into a flat to be near Daphne.

I don't think it was an easy decision for her to make, but circumstances forced it upon her. Keeping a fairly large house and garden, with only a little help, was a burden at her age. She could not rely on her children to do all that was necessary.

Ray had a great deal on his mind at this time. I was so proud of him when Benderdales opened and the photocopying business became such an overnight success that he had found it necessary to employ an assistant. He was not able to devote enough time to the clearing out of his mother's house. With her agreement, it was let furnished. Daphne and Len found her a comfortable flat in a new complex near to them. She took what furniture she needed and settled in, sad, but relieved.

An agent was employed to oversee the financial arrangements regarding the letting of the house and for a while life's problems were solved on that front.

My parents had sold my old home, piano and all, and had moved into sheltered accommodation in the same town. I was keen to support them both, but travelling up and down to the coast by train was tiresome. The remainder of my aunt's legacy was used to buy a Mini. I cannot say how much I appreciated the freedom it gave me.

The journey to the coast was not arduous at that time, there was not so much traffic on the roads as there is now. I knew the route without hesitation. Ray always avoided the busiest spots when he drove us down.

It was when I travelled alone, stopping overnight in the visitors' room at Trees, where my parents were comfortably settled, that I began to think about myself as a participant in the progress of time. Sometimes I felt in charge, but increasingly, I felt carried along with the unpredictable life changes of those around me.

When I returned from a weekend away to see my parents on one occasion, Alice came bounding down the stairs to greet me in a state of high excitement. Her Auntie Daphne and Uncle Len were planning a holiday in Paris and they had offered to take her with them if Ray and I agreed. She would need more pocket money, she said. Ray was never keen to travel abroad, he didn't like to be far away from the new business. This was a wonderful opportunity for Alice to visit the Louvre and other art galleries, which Daphne had promised they would do.

We were Mum and Dad, so of course she knew beforehand we would agree to her going. She gave us both a hug and was radiantly happy. At the time I had a passing wish that I would like to go too, but I was needed at home. It was holiday time for my pupils and I was able to practise in an empty house for a while. At this time, I had been asked to join the string quartet in a work they were performing at a concert later in the year, a chance to meet Hannah, as she always attended their concerts with her son.

Ray and I looked for the post each morning during Alice's absence abroad. Sure enough, when we were giving up hope of receiving a card from her, just before she was due home, one arrived. It had taken a week to come and she had not yet been to the art galleries. Her news though, left me absolutely amazed.

A family staying at the same hotel had noticed the name Benderdale in the register. Daphne and Len had signed in as Foster, and Alice, of course, in her name. On enquiring, they made contact in the lounge of the hotel after supper on their first evening. They introduced themselves as William and Philippa Strange and daughter, Janet. Neither Daphne nor Len knew who they were, but when they showed their delight at meeting Alice, a connection was made and a lively conversation ensued.

I couldn't wait for Alice to return to tell me all about this remarkable coincidence. Alice had made lasting friends with Janet, she told me. They had visited the art galleries, Notre Dame Cathedral, the Eiffel Tower and had been to an opera at Opera Comique, the latter especially for Philippa. William and Len had gone off on their own, having found much in common. Daphne and Philippa had escorted the girls wherever they wanted to go. Young Christopher, Janet's brother, was now grown up, an independent adult and not with them.

I gathered it was a fond farewell for all parties when the time came for them to come home. After a long telephone call with Philippa, I promised to drive to the Norfolk coast with Alice before their long school holiday was over.

Ray could see how keen I was to spend some time away. He had managed when I had driven to the south coast. Alice was good company for him and helped in the kitchen, but at this suggestion we decided to ask his mother to come and keep him company whilst we were away. I was sure she would welcome the chance to spend time with her son, and indeed it proved to be the case.

Chapter 22

The reaction I had at meeting Philippa again surprised me, an uncontrollable emotion of love and affection for her was overwhelming, and tears came to my eyes. They were excused by laughter and soon wiped away as I greeted William and Janet.

Alice was well known to them. The two girls disappeared quickly for a tour of the house and garden on their own.

It was mid-morning and coffee time. Sitting in the lounge among familiar pieces of furniture, with a cup in my hand, I felt more in control of myself. We were older and time had left its mark in that we had all put on weight and both Philippa and I were beginning to grow grey hairs, but we had too much to talk about to mention that.

Their chance meeting with Daphne and Len had been fortuitous, an answer to the concern they had about Janet who, in her teens, had been finding life difficult and needed a distraction. She had taken after her father in that she had grown in height beyond her peers at school. She was quite slim and rather self-conscious. Alice was a good height and the difference between them was not so pronounced when they were together. Alice's hair was auburn as was mine, and she stood out at school because of that — she took it in her stride when any impertinent comment was made.

Philippa and William had wondered, as Ray and I had done on our last holiday, if this special time together in Paris might not be the last holiday Janet would want to accompany them. Her brother, Christopher, spent his holidays with his friends, visiting his parents as a loving duty.

Meeting with Daphne and Len gave more purpose to their time abroad, they were delighted to see Alice and Janet enjoying each other's company. There was so much for us to talk about. Philippa had not been kept informed regarding the selling of the old premises of Benderdales — one doesn't write that sort of news on a Christmas card — although Daphne had said she mentioned the opening of the High Street business when they were in Paris.

I wished Ray had been with us and could have conversed with William about the effort the whole process had taken. Len had probably outlined the main family news, with his comments, no doubt. I was very proud of my husband; there were not many opportunities for me to talk about his achievements, but I spoke of the new flourishing business with pride. It wasn't as if Philippa had not known him at the old premises.

When William retired to his study — his private hide-a-way — Philippa and I had talked of our ventures into the music world since we last met. She was surprised when I said I had been in touch with Hannah whom she had known quite well from her choir days. The chance of my returning to accompany the choir had not surfaced again, so my news about them was second-hand. I could only highlight my occasional performances with the quartet and the piano pupils I still taught then.

Philippa had felt fulfilled when she sang in the choir and was its secretary, but since Janet was born and their move to Norfolk, she had not been able to continue her singing.

Talking about it brought some of my frustration to the surface and I felt I had not made the most of opportunities which may have been there for me. It seemed we both had our memories, but I scolded myself as appearing ungrateful for the loving and secure family life I had, and quickly dismissed any negative thoughts.

I only saw Alice at meal times. Both girls were intelligent and artistic. William had given Janet a camera for her previous birthday, and a new world had opened up for her. Alice was drawn into Janet's enthusiasm, and sure enough a camera was at the top of her most wanted list.

Philippa and I had renewed our friendship and we both agreed that we would not let it lapse again.

Chapter 23

We had just finished lunch one Saturday, rather late, as Ray had been playing golf, when the telephone rang. My immediate thought was Alice, keeping us up to date now she was away studying; her evenings were often full of college activities and she rang at odd times. But it was Daphne, asking if she could come and see us. I had guessed what it was about.

Vi had settled well in her flat, managing to look after herself in a quiet undemanding way, keen to preserve her independence. However she was becoming less mobile.

Time had not stood still for Daphne either, and she was finding the travelling to her work in London tiring on top of holding a senior position at the firm for which she worked. She and Len had reaped the benefit of successful careers over the years, they were both looking forward to their retirement when each would draw a comfortable pension.

Ray's life was Benderdales in the High Street. He had moved with the times and been successful too. Long holidays had been few and far between — abroad never. Retirement was not an option yet.

At this time, with Alice away studying, I was able to contribute more to our finances. I had been fortunate enough to find a part-time peripatetic post at two senior schools in the borough, my private pupils had moved on. I was pleased to be working.

My own parents, in their eighties, were very much on my mind. It had been a sensible move to sell the house a few years ago. They had lived quietly too, enjoying the fresh sea air, taking exercise together and joining the social activities organised at Trees. Mum even played the piano for them when the residents had a musical morning. After visiting them I always left amazed at how well they looked considering their great age.

Daphne drove over to see us and as I expected, her mother was the reason for her visit.

Ray and I had been looking in on Vi almost every weekend, taking it in turns to make sure she had everything she needed. Daphne or Len also called in during the week after work, they lived close enough to walk to the flat. They liked to keep most weekends free to drive to the cottage they had recently bought in the country. They considered undertaking long walks, enjoying fresh air, was essential after a week working in London.

It seemed everyone was enjoying the outdoors. Perhaps I should make a point of doing the same instead of staying in so much practising, I had thought.

The problem confronting us was that Vi had moved into a second floor flat, and she felt she was becoming housebound, as the stairs were presenting a problem for her. There was no lift in the building, consequently she wanted to move to be on the ground floor.

We put our heads together. It was a pressing problem which had rather crept up on us. Ray and I had taken Vi out in the car occasionally for a change of scene, but we now realised the ability to walk to the corner shop, with the aid of her stick, or to the friendly chapel, where there was a weekly social gathering, was absolutely essential for her wellbeing. Whilst she was still able to do it, we felt we must hasten her move. It was a pity we had not considered the likelihood of this problem arising, but at the time, Vi was so anxious to move from the family home that we had been happy to find a flat near Daphne. I remembered later on how Peg in de Prinz Road was confined to her one room. I should have brought her experience to mind when Vi first moved. Unfortunately I did not. It was possible that a ground floor flat would become vacant in the future, but we could not wait for one in the same building.

On further investigation, not far away, another block of flats was being built on land once occupied by a large, rather ugly Victorian house, which had been demolished. The plans showed the installation of a lift for those not quick enough to sign up for a flat on the ground floor. We decided to apply promptly, even though it would be six months before Vi was able to move in. But all went well, and within a year Vi was happily settled again.

A month or two and more may go by, lulling one into thinking that time has slowed down to a gentle saunter, and the routine of life will continue uninterrupted into the future, too far ahead for us to be concerned about.

Chapter 24

In the first months of the New Year, changes in our life came initially from Vi, with the news that Vicky was getting married and moving to Spain with her second husband, Harold. It was a popular choice at the time for couples to live out their retirement in a sunny climate, away from the cold unpredictable weather which was often our lot.

Vicky made a special effort to visit Vi with her unexpected news and to say good bye. She went without coming to see Ray and me, but Vi explained that she had left an invitation for us to visit Harold and herself in Spain. I knew Alice would be sad, as she was very fond of Vicky, although her life was opening out with new friends and she had plenty to occupy her time at college.

Vicky and I had little in common, nevertheless I found I would miss her outgoing nature, and her flashy style, so different in character from Philippa. I was pleased that she had found happiness with Harold, but I doubted we would travel to Spain to see them.

However, I had left Alice out of the equation; it wasn't long before she told us of her plans to visit

Vicky during her long vacation from college. A request for the necessary euros could not be refused. It was after all part of her education, we concluded. She was enjoying opportunities life had not offered to Ray and me.

Philippa's daughter Janet had begun making photography her career. Her college days were over and with her passion for taking pictures of everyday life, she found Alice's invitation to accompany her to Spain, irresistible.

And so, they went together. Ray and I, William and Philippa, waited patiently for the picture postcards to arrive on the door mat, very grateful for the phone calls from Vicky telling us of their safe arrival. Lucky Vicky, I thought, able to spoil Alice for a few days. I was beginning to treasure the times when Alice was home relaxing with us. I watched as she matured into a confident young lady, developing her obvious talent for design.

On their return Janet spent the night with us before returning to Norfolk, and we heard all about the idyllic surroundings where Vicky had settled with her husband Harold.

Later that year I received a phone call from Philippa, always a pleasant surprise, although this time her news delighted me one minute and saddened me the next. The family were returning to London to live. William was in need of treatment at one of the major hospitals, and it was not likely they would return to Norfolk. Details were few, but I knew Philippa would keep me up to date. Pleased as I was at their return, I wished it had not been for such a reason.

That same year the next major change in our lives came one hot sunny day in August. I was sitting out in the garden under an apple tree we had planted years ago when we first moved in, and were now grateful for the shade it gave.

Ray was due back from work and I listened for his car driving up to the garage door, a sign for me to attend to supper. He would be hungry after working later than usual to complete an order. Over our meal we sat talking about the news on the television, as one does when something important happens in this country or around the world. He enquired if I had heard news from his mother, who often phoned, or from Alice. He was silent after my reply in the negative, finishing his supper, head down.

When I rose to clear the dishes away, he stopped me, and asked me to sit down again as he wanted to tell me something. I sensed that it was important by his serious tone. "What now?" I thought.

"I've had an offer for the business," he said. With raised eyebrows and mouth open, I stared at him. How tired he was looking, and I wondered if I had been missing the effects on him of his constant commitment. For a minute or two I studied the empty dishes I had returned to the table.

"Goodness," was all I could say.

This was another life changing moment for him, a new situation where all responsibility rested on his shoulders. His father was not there this time to offer advice.

"It has come out of the blue," he said, "and I shall have to think seriously about it."

I went quickly round the table, putting my arms around his shoulders and kissing him. I dearly loved this most warm-hearted and unselfish man. I knew Benderdales was thriving, Ray had kept pace with the advancing technology, it was financially sound, and he had worked tirelessly for years.

He continued to share his thoughts with me and I listened intently. I had guessed he did not intend working as long as his father had done. At present he put in long hours, taking few holidays of any length. Another consideration was the fact that Alice would not wish to continue the business after he retired. With the ups and downs of the economy, it would be in his best interest to sell if times were favourable. "I have to be realistic," he had said. He was aware that his aged mother and Daphne would certainly need to be informed if he decided to go ahead with the sale.

I had found it difficult to engage with the financial and legal side of his family affairs. I felt somewhat side-lined when Alfred's legacy had been finally distributed, taking it for granted that Ray would continue with the business, and Vi would inherit her husband's estate. Life would go smoothly, day to day routine adjusting gradually as Alice grew up, weeks lived and left behind in quick succession.

This new challenge for Ray and all the ramifications another sale would entail, filled me with dread. I found it unsettling as I tried to look into the future. Would he retire early? Would we have to move? I felt it was a moment for me to wake up and take serious notice of the decisions we would soon have to make, to try to foresee changes and be prepared.

My thoughts led me to consider my own situation regarding the future of my parents. I could not expect Ray to involve himself in the affairs of my side of the family. It began to play on my mind. I had to sort out my position before I could concentrate on Ray's financial challenges, which ultimately affected me.

"It would be sensible," Ray said, when I brought up the subject, saying that I planned to visit my mother and father. I hoped that the news of the sale of Benderdales would be a starting point, leading to the subject of their provision for each other. It was a delicate subject.

Chapter 25

The traffic was quite heavy driving down to the coast, at one stage the queue of cars built up, finally coming to a halt. We remained stationary for quite a while. Mum and dad knew I was coming to see them and I was afraid they would be anxious by the delay.

I sat thinking on the possibility of my mother not being able to stay at Trees due to lack of funds, if father's pension stopped at his death. I decided that I would be quite willing to give up my part time teaching to care for her. But would she want to be moved to live with Ray and me, leaving her seaside town and her friends there?

It was as well the traffic moved on and I could concentrate on my driving. I made good progress to the coast, arriving in time for lunch. I was always made welcome by the staff who were expecting me.

The residents preferred to eat quietly, as did my parents. Most of the elderly people found it difficult to hear when several conversations were being carried on at once. Our greeting was brief as I accompanied them into the dining room.

After an hour's rest, during which time I brought mum and dad up to date, first with greetings from Ray, then with news of Alice and the college course on fabric design and printing she had chosen to study, and also news of Vi, and of Vicky. They were very sad to hear that William was ill, and recalled the happy evening they spent with him and Philippa years ago.

Having the car at their disposal, it was planned that I should drive them to a spot along the coast which we knew well, and perhaps, if they felt like it, we could walk along the promenade. It was a lovely warm afternoon, there were plenty of seats where we could stop, rest and admire the view of sea and sky. I loved to do so, for living miles inland it was a great pleasure to breathe the pure sea air.

They were happy moments, which I have always treasured, for unbeknown to me then, it was the last time we would be together, out enjoying ourselves.

Walking slowly along the front, with my mother going ahead to occupy a vacant seat, I mentioned to my father that in all probability Ray would be selling the business, as he had received an interesting enquiry from a would-be purchaser. I was concerned as to how it would leave us financially until we in our turn would become pensioners.

"We sold our house, and had always lived within our means," said my father, and before I could ask further, he continued, "your mother is cared for at Trees if I should go first. All arrangements are made," he added with a smile. "You have no need to worry about anything," he said, as he put his arm around me.

How wise my father was to discern my anxiety, putting me at ease. My life had been dominated with the care of Ray, my husband, and of my daughter, Alice, having music always knocking on the door for attention. I had a deep love for my parents who always had my best interest at heart, releasing me to freedom in the enticing world, when I was still a teenager.

My father thought well of Ray. He assured me that he would seek good advice before taking such a step, and professional help if he decided to sell the business. He said he was sorry that he could not help, as so much in the legal and financial world had changed since his day.

"Of course, I understand," I said, remembering the expertise my father had throughout his working life, and now not relevant.

We caught up with my mother and all sat looking out to sea. It was as if I was ten years old, and dad had driven us over for the afternoon, mum was going to produce a thermos of tea, some sandwiches and homemade fruit cake, and I was going into the sea to paddle.

I hugged and kissed them before setting out in the early evening for home and Ray. Alice would be phoning later on. My mind rested quietly as I deviated to drive past my old home before joining the main road northward. I was eighteen when I left there for college. Mum and dad had not seen very much of me since my marriage. Their occasional trips to stay briefly with us, before the journey got too much for them, and my short visits, which seemed over before they had begun, left me feeling a little sad.

terms of her will. I knew that Ray was aware that his father had given him money, as a down payment on the house. the value of the business had risen, and an indication of the settlement, would be helpful as he planned to retire after the sale. I sensed that Len was interested in the distribution too. I had been prepared to grasp the financial implications of Ray selling the business, but coupled with the distribution of the legacy, I mentally retreated. Ray could not avoid his obligations and I wondered if I would be able to offer the support he really needed.

Len would be there for Daphne, giving of his experience in matters of this kind. Daphne herself would feel quite capable of understanding all the legalities.

When Len spoke of the will, I had replied that I was sure Alfred had guided Vi years ago, and that Ray would be in contact with their solicitor. Len agreed with me.

We eventually prepared to leave for home. Ray would need to arrange his timetable with his assistant Kevin, in order for him to visit the family solicitor. Daphne undertook to deal with her mother's personal things and I was pleased to offer my help in that.

For the moment, the sale of Benderdales was on hold and nothing was said to Daphne and Len.

When Ray had done all that was necessary, he made an appointment with the family solicitor. He was relieved to find that his mother had made a will. She had also appointed an executor, and that surprised Ray. Vi had been very aware that running his business was a full time job. She had lived through the stresses and strains when Alfred was responsible for dead-lines, and that had not changed with the modern printing business. She had thought to make life as straightforward as possible for Ray, when drawing up her will.

What was news to Ray, was that the executor his mother had chosen, was the existing tenant of the Benderdale family home. The financial side of the let had run very smoothly in the hands of the agent. Ray and Daphne did not know that their tenant, Sir James J, a retired diplomat from overseas, and living alone with a housekeeper, had welcomed occasional visits from Vi. She had been very keen to oversee the upkeep of the large garden which almost surrounded the corner house. He was pleased she showed an interest.

Vi had loved returning to her former home, half furnished with things she recognised, half furnished with items the retired gentleman had brought with him. In fact, they had become friends over the years. Vi had been grateful that she could talk to someone of experience, outside the family.

She had been an intelligent woman, but had not had the opportunity to further her education.

Ray had met Sir James when arrangements for the tenancy had been agreed, but all contact afterwards had been through the agent. It was accepted that he should live out his retirement in the old family home.

Surprised as both Ray and Daphne were, they agreed with the solicitor's instructions, and left all the intricacies of the taxes due on the estate, to him to deal with, as was required.

Chapter 27

Vicky telephoned a few days before the funeral to ask if she could stay with us beforehand. She would be flying over from Spain on her own the day before and would return the day after. I wasn't at all surprised that she came on her own. At first I didn't recognise her — it was the occasion of course — dressed smartly in black, but with little of the rather liberal cosmetics I was used to seeing her wear. She had entered middle age. Alice, home from college, greeted her lovingly.

Philippa and Janet were coming to a buffet lunch before the afternoon service. Both Ray and I had arranged a few days away from work to concentrate on our guests. There seemed to be a hundred and one details for me to attend to, taking on the responsibilities as host, on this sad occasion. My parents were too frail to come.

I was surprised how many people attended Vi's funeral, especially the number of relatives who came. Ray and Daphne greeted cousins they had not seen since childhood. Names on Christmas cards had suddenly come to life. I was solemnly introduced to each one, but none were called

Benderdale. It was the first time I had heard anyone call Ray's mother, Auntie. They had travelled down from Yorkshire. Vi's family had extended northward into Durham too, so over the years it had been difficult to meet together.

Several customers who had known Alfred and Ray were present, and I recognised folk from the flats where Vi had recently made her home.

Sir James came, knowing no one apart from Ray, who introduced him to Daphne, Len, myself and Alice. He sat with us, and afterwards at the refreshments in the hall of the chapel, where the service had been held, and from where Ray and Daphne had been driven on their own to Vi's final cremation. Sir James spoke to me of how much he would miss his dear friend. I was pleased to have Len and Alice with me to share in the conversation until Ray and Daphne returned, and grateful that their support allowed me to greet those who had stayed after the service, for the refreshments.

I was able to have a word with Hannah who came, remembering how Vi had looked after Alice while she had her piano lesson, and then stayed for coffee and a chat with Vi and me.

It was a quiet supper that evening. Philippa and Janet had driven home, taking Alice to the station, as she was anxious to return to college. Vicky was keen to tell us how she and Harold had met, saying how wonderful it was to have someone to love and care for her, and for her to have someone to love and care for. She had spent so many years in the fashion world, she had never regretted it, she said, but it was an exhausting way of life from which she was now quite willing to step away and look after Harold as he began his retirement.

She seemed a much calmer person. Both Ray and I felt relaxed in her company; we were her family and perhaps one day we would feel free to accept her invitation to fly to Spain and meet Harold. There had never been a closeness between her and Daphne. I suppose it was understandable, but now that Vi had gone, it was not impossible that Vicky and Harold would come back for a visit and we could all meet.

It was a real affectionate goodbye from Ray and myself when Vicky left early the next day for her flight back to Spain. Ray left for the business, and I had music lessons to give at school.

Later when Ray and I were alone, he told me that Sir James would shortly be giving notice to end his tenancy and be moving to where he could be assured of more care, as he was feeling his age, and wasn't quite so mobile as he used to be. Ray said that Daphne would be able to sell the property once he had gone.

Alice had been pleased when she heard that she had inherited her grandmother's jewellery, apart from one item of Daphne's choosing. I hoped that she would also keep one piece to remind her of her grandmother. None of it was the style Alice would wear herself, and I expected her to sell it. Vicky inherited a small amount of money which would not mean quite so much to her now she was married to Harold.

It took several months for the settlement of the will to be finalised, during which time Ray had been seeking advice over his proposed sale of the printing business. The prospective buyer had been quite willing to wait before pressing for a decision. I was relieved that was the case, as Ray felt the loss of his parents and the family associations.

He was kept well informed by Sir James of the rather complicated procedure relating to the wills. Sir James proved a most efficient executor, despite his age, he knew what he was doing and worked well with the family solicitor. Even so, it was nearly a year before Ray and Daphne finally received their inheritance, and Ray could turn his attention to the transferring of the printing business to a new owner.

What a year it had been. Philippa and William were settled back in North London, where William had made good progress following a major operation. Although he was not the upright man I first knew, he was able to enjoy his life in Philippa's good care. Not having Vi to visit, I was able to meet up with her, and we organised our lives to enable us to attend a few concerts together in London. How enjoyable that was, out of the demands of daily life, and into that other place of peaceful pleasure and mental massage.

Chapter 28

Ray and I will never know whose idea it was, but when Daphne and Len came to supper with us, a month or so after the inheritance was finally distributed, Daphne announced her intention to sell the Benderdale home to a builder. It came as a shock and for a minute or two we continued our meal in silence.

Of course, Daphne had every right to do what she wanted with her inheritance. We assumed that she would sell the property, benefitting from the steeply rising market, to someone who would make the house their home. I think Ray was looking forward to passing by, to see how well it was being cared for, and note if any alterations had been made by the new owners.

It was a house of happy memories for him, of the days when he worked with his father and they brought tricky printing problems home with them, to shut themselves away in the little room his father called his office, to sort them out.

The garden had childhood memories of summer days, playing football with his friends on the lawn, of camping out at night in the tent he had been given for his birthday one year, of firework nights with a bonfire, and hot soup and sausages brought out for them by his mother, as they watched the dying embers.

Len sat quietly as Daphne continued to say that she had received a good price from a builder, who planned to demolish the house and erect a block of flats similar to the ones her mother had moved to from the family home.

Ray was quiet, saying nothing apart from agreeing that she could do as she wished. However sad he felt inwardly, he did not remonstrate, but outlined his own plans to sell the shop in the High Street and retire in the near future.

"Benderdales has been such a well-known name in the district," I said, "it will be rather sad when it disappears." Both brother and sister were playing their part in it, I thought.

"Ah," said Daphne, "that won't be quite the case. I have stipulated to the builder, that when the flats are completed, the building will be called "Benderdale Court", and he will have to sign an agreement to that effect."

We both brightened at that, and it softened the shock of her news. The conversation turned to our coming retirement and the plans for the future, fully formed, or still looking at options.

After supper Daphne helped me clear away the dishes, saying how much she and Len had enjoyed their meal, stressing the great pleasure of having someone cook for them. That struck a chord with me, remembering my first efforts at entertaining years ago.

We had met several times at Vi's flat to organise the removal and disposal of her clothes and personal effects. Because she had moved twice in recent years Vi had reduced them to a minimum. She had been an avid reader, but used the local library rather than acquiring books herself. We arranged for her good quality furniture to be sold and the proceeds were shared with Ray.

In the evenings together, after work had finished for the day and there was just the two of us, Daphne and I conversed without interruption. I warmed to her more relaxed and confiding mood.

She had admitted to me that she wasn't as close to her mother as she might have been. Ray always seemed to come first, and then lively young Vicky was always about. Daphne admitted that when she came, being the younger and plainer of the two, she disappeared to her own bedroom and her books, and left Ray's older friends to themselves. She told me that she was secretly very pleased when Vicky married someone else, though she felt no unfriendliness towards her now.

When the dishwasher was full and left to do its work, we opened the back door and walked out into the garden. Our conversation continuing.

"Len and I realised that we wouldn't have a family. We immersed ourselves in our work," she said. "We've both been successful and now that I have inherited substantially from my father and mother, we are left in a very comfortable position." Then, her voice broke. "I did so want to have children, but with Len it was not possible; I couldn't live without him, he is everything I have now mum has gone," she said.

"Oh Daphne," I replied firmly, "No! you will always have our love and affection." And as I turned towards her, she burst into tears. I hugged her and was tearful too. Handkerchiefs out after a minute, and we stilled ourselves. From then on we felt confidingly comfortable in each other's company. I made an effort to move towards her rather than to retreat when her strong personality came to the fore.

Arm in arm we re-entered the dining room through the French windows, to find it empty. Voices came from the hall, and we found Ray and Len putting a golf ball the length of the hall into a practise hole.

"Len thinks he might take up golf," announced Ray. Daphne and I just stood still and laughed.

Chapter 29

Ray's attention was now drawn to the transference of the business. He had time to decide if this was really what he wanted to do. It seemed quite reasonable for him to think about retirement after so many years of devotion to Benderdales. He could look back with pride in being able to sell a going concern. He realised that what he had modernised a few years ago, was itself being superseded by new developments, and he didn't have the enthusiasm to renew the printers in the near future.

I tried to follow as he explained the need to engage a chartered accountant, experienced in chartered tax advice. It all seemed so complicated to me, even working out the actual date of transfer, to accord with tax relief. The very word *tax*, sent shivers up my spine. Bit by bit, necessary calculations were made and Ray seemed relaxed.

But just when he thought all was going smoothly, he came home one evening looking glum. When the property was being assessed, it was discovered that work needed doing on the roof to guarantee it remained watertight. The upstairs room was used as an office and a store, and signs of damp had been noticed. It was a blow, remedial work had to be done and paid for before the sale.

I looked worried, Ray drew me into his arms, assuring me that everything would work out, I was not to be concerned. "We could have done without it, nevertheless," I thought.

We were invited to have supper with Len and Daphne one evening. It was only natural for Daphne to tell us about the completion of the sale of the family home, and the preparations for the demolition.

"We are nearly there," said Ray, "we need some building work done on the roof of the premises, and then we will be home and dry," he added with a quiet laugh. "I shall not be sorry to have more time to enjoy life."

It was a pleasant change for us to be entertained. Daphne proved to be a good cook, she seemed relaxed and made us feel at home. She and I found plenty to talk about. She was always interested in Alice's progress, and she showed a tenderness in asking after my parents who were now very frail and in their nineties. And my Ray spoke to Len, who showed a keen interest in the complicated process in selling the business.

As we drove home, Ray remarked that they had enjoyed each other's company. Both had had years of concentrating on their work, which had left no space for them to be alone together for long, in a manly tête-à-tête. Ray met friends at the golf club, but I did not know of Len having interests outside his work and the home. We needed this closeness now that Alfred and Vi were gone. After all, we were family, and there weren't many of us. Len was an only child with no relations of whom he had ever spoken. Daphne had never mentioned any. I liked to think that Alice had an auntie and an uncle, being an only child herself.

Chapter 30

Retirement eventually came for Ray and also for me. Now that he was home I had willingly given up my piano teaching at the schools, and also my association with the quartet, not that I had stopped playing. We managed perfectly well financially, and enjoyed our freedom.

In the years that followed Vi's death, I grieved at the loss of my parents, and their quiet passing left me with a time of sadness.

We did not move; by the time Ray had retired, he had paid off the mortgage on the house, and to our satisfaction we watched the housing market rise in leaps and bounds. We lived in a quiet residential area where houses such as ours became very desirable.

Ray enjoyed getting our wild garden under control and generally improving the house, inside and out, with his expertise in DIY. All in all, with his regular golf, he became much fitter and was quite content.

Alice, after her degree, joined a group of textile designers in the Midlands. Ray and I watched anxiously, as she moved away to find a flat of her own near her work, to live an independent life, as I had done many years ago. No bedsit with a Mrs Dean for a landlady, though. How we missed her; her comings and goings, her hurried meals to be out in time to meet friends, her lazy days — how few they were — when she was at home doing this and that. I was helpless to prevent the years rolling by, too busy to pause and drink in the pleasure of her company when I had appointments to keep for teaching and playing.

Yes, I would have liked her to be musical and to appreciate the life which gave me great pleasure and satisfaction, but then, I realised she had talents inherited from her father and I was very proud of her achievements. I loved her, and her happiness was all I wanted. Our mum and daughter times together were treasured.

Philippa and I often met. She sang and I accompanied her. Hannah had time to pursue her piano playing and we met to play duets. It was perfect heaven when the three of us came together to make music. We began to be so proficient in our performance that we put ourselves forward to entertain in aid of local charities.

And Vicky? We didn't meet again. Her life was devoted to Harold who would not travel back to this country. Ray was not keen to travel abroad either. Alice visited her when she and Janet went to Spain on holiday.

As I put down the pen at the end of my story, I glanced at the date. It was the sixth of August. It will be the seventh tomorrow, I noted, dear Maudie, not forgotten.